I0690115

THE RISE OF THE GRAY GHOST

Michael Aye

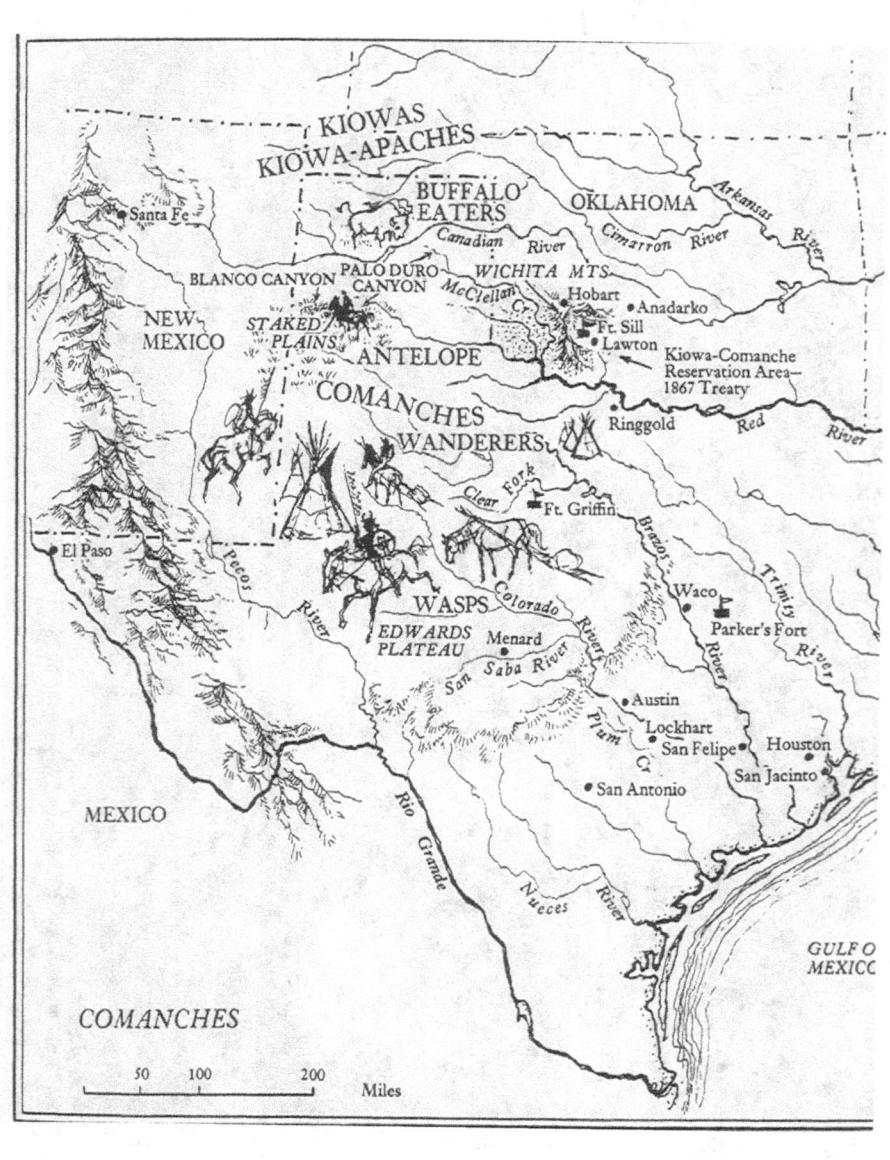

KIOWAS
KIOWA-APACHES
BUFFALO EATERS
OKLAHOMA
Arkansas
Santa Fe
Canadian   River   Cimarron   River   River
BLANCO CANYON   PALO DURO   WICHITA MTS.
CANYON   McClellan   Hobart
NEW   STAKED   Cr.   Anadarko
MEXICO   PLAINS   ANTELOPE   Ft. Sill
        Lawton
COMANCHES   Kiowa-Comanche
WANDERERS   Ringgold   Reservation Area—
        1867 Treaty
        Red   River
Clear Fork   Ft. Griffin
        Braxos
El Paso   Colorado   Waco
WASPS   River   Trinity
Pecos   EDWARDS   Menard   Parker's Fort
        PLATEAU   San Saba River   River
River   Austin   River
        Lockhart
        San Felipe   Houston
        San Antonio   San Jacinto

MEXICO
        Rio Grande

        Nueces   River   GULF O
        MEXICO

COMANCHES

50   100   200
        Miles

THE RISE

OF THE

GRAY GHOST

Michael Aye

BITINGDUCK PRESS
ALTADENA, CA

Published by Boson Books
An imprint of Bitingduck Press
ISBN 978-1-68553-011-2
eISBN 978-1-68553-007-5
© 2022 Michael Fowler
All rights reserved
For information contact
Bitingduck Press, LLC
Altadena, California
notifications@bitingduckpress.com
http://www.bitingduckpress.com

Cover art by Mike Benton
https://mike-benton.pixels.com/

Header and title font, "Serial Publication"
http://www.kcfonts.com/

# Books by Michael Aye

THE FIGHTING ANTHONYS SERIES
The Reaper, Book One
H.M.S. SeaWolf, Book Two
Barracuda, Book Three
SeaHorse, Book Four
Peregrine, Book Five
Trident, Book Six
Leopard, Book Seven
Ares, Book Eight
Andalucia, Book 9

WAR 1812 TRILOGY
War 1812, Remember the Raisin, Book One
War 1812, Battle at Horseshoe Bend, Book Two
War 1812, Battle of New Orleans, Book Three

PYRATE TRILOGY
Pyrate, The Rise of Cooper Cain, Book One
Pyrate, Letter of Marque, Book Two
Pyrate, The Hunter, Book 3

SMUGGLERS
The Smugglers of Deal, Book One

PROLOGUE

WHAT SOUNDED LIKE DISTANT THUNDER *that morning was closer, much closer. The Battle of Chickamauga would go down in history as the bloodiest two days in American history, but that mattered little to Major Will Lee, senior surgeon in General Bragg's Confederate army. What did matter was the mounting number of wounded that the stretcher bearers were bringing in. There were so many that Lee had Shad, a freed slave, doing what he could to triage the wounded. Several had died before they could be seen, and more would follow. The morphine and laudanum had long since run out. The only pain relief left was brandy and several jugs of rot-gut moonshine. Shad had been instructed to liberally give the shine to those too far gone to help.*

BOOM...BOOM...BOOM!! *The cannon fire continued to thunder away, and the ground inside the surgery tent seemed to shake as each gun fired. The battle was much closer now. Will heard the high pitched yells and curses easily as they interlaced with the rapid firing of muskets. The smoke of battle drifted toward the field hospital and soon the surgical tent was a fog. The acrid smell of gun powder filled the nostrils and burned the eyes of the surgeons and volunteers. The volunteers* consisted of some nurses, and others who had no medical training but felt it was their Christian duty to help the wounded, regardless of the man's uniform...blue or gray. Both ends of the tent were opened, and they hoped it would clear out the smoke. The surgeon was coughing, making it very difficult to operate.

A messenger from General Bragg galloped up on a lathered horse. "Evacuate the wounded," he shouted. "The Yanks are just over the rise and closing fast." The messenger's words were punctuated by a cannon ball that passed through the top of the tent.

"Hold your hand here," Lee ordered the nurse helping him.

She placed a dirty sponge on top of a bleeder that was pumping blood out from an artery in the soldier's groin. A bayonet wound, she thought.

Lee turned to the other surgeons, "Finish what you can and move the wounded out of here."

There was another boom and another hole in the tent, this one lower. The surgeons and helpers moved as quickly as possible.

Shad ran into the tent. "We have three wagons and mules," he gasped.

"Three," Lee hissed, thinking that was hardly enough for the ones who'd just been operated on. "Find a sergeant in the walking wounded, Shad. Have him get those who can walk up and marching. Otherwise..." The otherwise was understood, and nobody wanted to be in a Yankee prison camp. Most of the soldiers would prefer death.

Lee was almost run over by retreating Confederate soldiers as he went back to his patient with the bayonet wound in the groin. When Lee got to the patient, he saw that the nurse was still applying pressure to the bleeder. Thank goodness the man had passed out due to shock. Would he recover once the bleeding was stopped? Only God knew.

Lee used a fairly clean scalpel and opened the wound. He removed, with forceps, some cloth that had come from the man's britches and also some grass. He poured water and then whiskey into the wound. He had clamped the bleeder with forceps and now tied a ligature around it, stopping the bleeding. The battle outside the tent was in a wild frenzy, as Lee started to close the wound. He'd just put in the third stitch when a Minie ball punctuated the tent and hit the nurse in the arm. It was like a swarm of balls piercing the white canvas as Lee knelt down. Thinking if they were outside and could be seen, then maybe, hopefully, the firing would be directed elsewhere.

Leaning over, Major Will Lee, surgeon of the Confederate Army, reached out to grasp the wounded nurse's arm. As he did, a cannon ball whooshed through the tent, taking his right hand off at the wrist. Will looked at the stump as blood spurted from the severed arteries. He wondered to himself, How am I going to operate now? Thankfully, everything went black and Will fainted.

Shad looked in horror as Lee fell. He grabbed a belt from a dead soldier and made a tourniquet. He then raced over and took a red hot iron from the burning coals and singed the stump. He cut off part of Lee's white coat, and after smearing the stump with bacon fat from a nearby cook fire, he wrapped the stump. He then hefted Lee on his back and ran in the direction that he'd seen the other Confederates run. The guns and cannons continued to blaze away behind him, but he didn't look back. He had to get Will to a surgeon. He was too good a man to let die. He knew the next field hospital was not too far. There, Will would get proper treatment, so he ran; never did he think to stop. No, he had to keep moving. Will's life depended on it.

It was some days later before Shad was told that General Bragg's army defeated the Yankee General Rosecrans. The South may have won the battle, he thought, but they lost the best surgeon in the army when Will Lee was wounded.

CHAPTER ONE

I T WAS MAY, 1865. WILL Lee sat in the swing at the end of the
porch in the shade of a large oak tree. He was drinking tea...
well, tea mixed with bourbon. He'd spent most of his days in this
same spot since being released from the hospital and the army. At
night, when he could no longer walk or stand up by himself, Shad
would help him up and to his room, undress him and put his friend
to bed.

Eagle Trace was a plantation near Wooten Station in Lee County,
Georgia. This area of Georgia had been untouched by the savagery
of war. Cotton was still the main crop. It would be taken to Albany
and floated down the Flint River on a barge to be sold to European
markets. That wasn't Will's concern, though. It was his brother
Brandon's area. He had been the farmer in the family, and Will was
a surgeon...had been a surgeon.

A has been, Will thought as he took another swallow of his tea
laced with bourbon. *A worthless has been. My future was gone in the
blink of an eye.* He recalled the looks...the pitying looks of the doctors, nurses, and orderlies at the hospital where he'd recovered...

recovered physically, at least. Neither the drugs at the hospital, nor the whiskey that he'd drank since coming home could drown his mental anguish. His career, his life was forever changed by a damnable cannon ball. He wasn't even sure if it had been the Yankees' ball or one of theirs from the way the battle had raged. What was for certain was that he was now nothing more than a worthless has been. It would have been better had Shad not saved him and had let him die. Now all he could do is sit on the porch of his home place and try to drown his sorrow.

Eagle Trace had been in the Lee family since the early 1800's. The family was part of the Lee's from Thunderbolt, Georgia. Their great-grandfather had fought with Andy "by Gawd" Jackson, and his father had fought with Washington. Will and Brandon's father had lived a peaceful life, only to die from heart failure in his sleep. Their mother had followed two years later.

Will could see a horse and rider coming down the lane. He knew from the slouched way the rider sat in the saddle that it was Chandler, Chan to his friends, Calhoun. He was a boyhood friend and now a barrister.

Chan swung down, giving the reins of his horse to a stable boy, and blurted out, "The war is over. Lee surrendered to Grant in April."

Damn, Lee thought, *all the useless slaughter for nothing.*

Chan stepped between two dogs and walked across the porch to the swing. He caught a whiff of alcohol on Will's breath. "My God, Will, it's not even noon yet and you reek. It's been nearly two years since you came home and all you do is sit and drink yourself into a stupor."

"What am I supposed to do?" Will growled, holding up his stump.

"You want the world to pity Will Lee because he lost a hand. You, at least, are home," Chan swore. "There're a lot of our friends that didn't make it back."

"I was a surgeon, though," Will flared back, waving his stump at his friend.

Chan responded back, "And now you're not, but you can still be a doctor."

"I have no interest in being a doctor," Will said.

"Be something else then...anything, find something," Chan replied. He surprised Will then by slapping the glass out of his hand. It landed in the yard, next to an azalea bush. "Shad," Chan yelled. "Shad."

"Yes sir."

"Shad, if he asks for another drink before sundown, tell him to get it himself. If he doesn't like it, you come to see me, I can use you."

"Yes sir," Shad replied smiling.

Chan paused and then spoke again, "I thought you'd made a hand for Will."

"I did, Mr. Chan. I even fitted it when he was passed out. It's a fine looking hand too."

Chan turned back to Will. "More, oh woe is me. Shad's made you a hand and you won't wear it."

"It's brown. I don't want a brown hand."

"Put a glove on it then. You can do that, can't you? You can get any blasted color you desire. Shad, I'm having a group of friends over tonight. Make sure that Will is dressed and sober and at my house at seven. Put the hand on him also."

"Yes sir," Shad replied as Chan stormed off.

WHILE WILL WAS DRESSING FOR the get-together that night, he saw that Brandon was dressing as well. He realized that this must be a planned business meeting and that Chan had included him to get him up and out of the house.

Shad came into the room and noticed Will was only partially dressed. "You better hurry, Mr. Will."

"Why?" Will snapped.

"Because Mr. Chandler and Miz Jen are expecting you." Shad paused a minute and then added, "Yo mama and daddy never raised you to be rude. I don't 'spect that they like looking down from heaven and seeing how you take on either."

"What would you know, Shad, you have all of your limbs," Will growled. "You've nothing to complain about."

Shad looked at Will. He had been somewhat of a companion to the man while growing up and then his personal servant for years. He'd only been freed when the war broke out. Will had wanted his slave...his confidant to live a life of his choosing. He'd been a slave until then; a well treated slave to be sure...but a slave.

Shad, thinking of Will's comments, looked at him in the eye, "Have you ever thought what it's like to be a slave, Mr. Will?"

Shad's words shook Will. He looked at his lifelong companion and said, "No, I haven't, Shad." The two men continued to look at each other for a while. "I'm sorry, Shad, please forgive me for my actions. It won't happen again."

Shad smiled, "Shucks, Mr. Lee, I knew that you'd come around in time. Now, let's be putting this hand on you."

Shad's hand was a truly a remarkable contraption. He had carved out an unbelievable likeness of a human hand. It was basically the same size of Will's left hand. He'd hollowed out the wrist section of the hand for the stump to fit into and placed cotton padding in it to keep down the rubbing and chafing. A leather harness was attached so that the artificial hand could be connected to the arm.

"Damn, Shad, how were you able to achieve such a good fit?" Will asked, letting loose with a rare curse.

"It took several tries," Shad admitted.

"When?" Will asked, as his surgeon's eye marveled at Shad's work.

"Mostly when you were dead drunk," Shad responded, smiling. Will, seeing the smile, couldn't contain himself and burst out laughing.

They were still laughing when Brandon walked into his brother's room. "Thank you, Lord, you've answered my prayers," he whispered.

***

WHEN WILL AND BRANDON ARRIVED at the Calhoun house, several carriages waited in the shade of the oaks. A stable boy took the horses while the men climbed the steps to the house. A liveried footman, at the front door, greeted the brothers and took their hats. They were led into a large room where several men were gathered. The brothers knew all but two as local neighbors from either Lee County or Albany. One of the two men that they didn't know wore the uniform of a ship's captain...with an empty sleeve.

This is why Chan invited me, Will thought, and then realized that it didn't anger him. Shaking hands with his neighbors was a bit awkward at first but not bad. Will smiled at his friends' gaffes and then had them smiling back. More than one slapped his back exclaiming how good it was to see him out and about. *What they didn't say*, Will thought, *was 'rather than in a drunken stupor.'*

The strangers were introduced as a British businessman from Liverpool, England, named David Hayes, and the sea captain as Macon Fallon. Fallon had been a blockade runner for the South and had made twenty-four successful runs before the blockade had gotten too tight, even for his ship, *The Falcon*.

After a hearty meal, brandy and cigars were broken out as the wives and daughters made their way to the sewing room. Will couldn't help but notice that his brother's eyes lingered on the sister of their neighbor's wife. Through his whiskey-sodden haze over the last two years, he'd recalled that the woman had only been married a short while when her husband had been killed in battle. *This might be something in the making for his brother*, he thought... he hoped. Will's thoughts were interrupted as Chan brought the meeting to order.

The southern United States had once been a major exporter of cotton. Word was that the north did not oppose the south regaining that recognition—money was needed to pay off the war debt. But what would it matter if the plantation owners profited as well. Mr. Hayes' company would offer a discount on shipping and a guaranteed rate on the cotton if an exclusive deal could be struck. Captain Fallon, a proven seaman, would command the ship transporting the cotton to England.

Will noticed, at one point during the meeting, that the captain was armed. The pistol was in a holster made to be drawn with his left hand. But it differed in that it was a cross draw rather than the conventional. He also noted that there was no flap on the holster like the army officers used and had a small thong fitted over the trigger. After the meeting, Will approached Captain Fallon and asked about the holster.

"Like you, I've lost an appendage," Fallon said. "The places that a sea captain finds himself are not always in the more reputable parts of town, and carrying a gun often keeps one out of trouble. I've found that I'm faster drawing across my body than pulling my gun in the usual manner, and when I need it, I usually need it in a hurry."

"Did you lose your arm in battle?" Brandon asked as he walked up, embarrassing Will somewhat.

"I apologize," Will said, eyeing his brother.

"Battle...yes; it was a battle of sorts," Captain Fallon replied. "I was engaged upon the field of honor under the oaks in New Orleans. A pistol ball shattered five inches of bone in the upper arm so it had to be amputated. The other gentleman was not so fortunate. My shot was dead center."

Brandon gave a little gasp, which caused Will to smile. Brandon was a Baptist minister when he wasn't farming. He'd never heard a shot fired in anger, so to be face-to-face with a man who had fought a duel was new ground.

Will looked at Macon Fallon and said, "I'd love for you to come out to Eagle Trace if you have the time, Captain. I'd like for my man to see your holster and develop one for me. Since the war things are not as peaceful as they were."

"I'd be glad to, Will, but drop the 'captain'. Call me 'Macon,' or even 'Fallon.' That's what most calls me."

Chan came up, at that time. "So you two are sharing tales. I shouldn't wonder," he said, smiling, and then added, "Mr. Hayes is going to stay over tonight so that we can go over these contracts. You are welcome to stay, Captain, or I can have you driven back to Albany."

"I've a better idea," Will threw out. "Why don't you come to Eagle Trace now? I will drive and tie our horses to the back of the carriage."

Smiling, Fallon agreed. "I assure you, sir, I'm most happy to accept. I've never been one for the paperwork."

CHAPTER TWO

T HE CARRIAGE RIDE WAS GOING along pleasantly. The moon was nearly full and the road was clearly marked in the moonlight. Brandon was saying that he'd invited Mr. and Mrs. Parsons, and Mrs. Parsons' sister, Gabby, to church Sunday and dinner afterwards.

"Beulah will have to cook up something special," Will said, as an armed rider rushed out from between some oak trees. The two horses pulling the carriage reared up and came down fighting the bit and reins.

"Hands in the air," the rider ordered. Seeing Fallon's pistol, he also said, "You...ever so slowly, with two fingers, pull out that pistol and drop it on the ground."

The man had moved his horse over to Fallon's side of the carriage to cover him better. "Now each of you, one at a time, reach for your wallet and toss it on the ground. When you've done that you can ride on. Preacher, you go first." *He knows us,* Will thought. Brandon did as ordered and then Will followed.

When Fallon reached into his coat, his hand came out with blazing speed. In his hand was not a wallet but a pistol. Flame shot from the end of the weapon, momentarily blinding everyone, but the ball ran true. The rogue grabbed his chest as he toppled backwards out of the saddle and on to the ground.

Brandon stared in shock. Will was astonished, "I've never seen anything like it. That was fast...fast and accurate."

Brandon was the first of the three men down. He was examining the man and said, "He's dead. You've killed him."

"Better him than us," Will replied. "He called you preacher, Brandon. He knew you, so he had to figure that we knew him. You don't think that he was going to let us go, do you?"

"I don't know," Brandon mumbled. "He said he would."

"He would have shot us in the back as we pulled off," Will answered. "You better thank God that we had Macon with us, Brandon, else there'd be no Sunday with Gabby."

The rest of the ride back to Eagle Trace was mostly silent, with the only conversation being when Will pointed out a boundary landmark. The stable boy met the carriage and whistled up some help.

Shad came down the steps to greet the men after seeing the carriage, when he'd expected only horses.

Will introduced Shad to Fallon saying, "This is Shad, named after Shadrach, Meshach, and Abednego in the Bible. It was my mother's idea. Shad and I have been...friends. He continued after a moment of thought, "We grew up together. Shad is a very talented man. It was he who made my hand."

Fallon then surprised everyone when he held out his left hand to shake Shad's hand. It was the first time that Will could recall a white man ever shaking a Negro's hand. It surprised Shad, as well, as he thrust out his hand to grasp Fallon's.

Brandon looked at Will and spoke, "I think I'll go in. You're going to notify Harvey, aren't you?"

Will nodded his answer. "Shad, take Caesar and go into Wooten Station and find Harvey. Tell him a highwayman attempted to rob us on the old stagecoach road. He was shot dead, as he was armed and we feared for our lives. The body is about three miles back at the oaks."

When Shad left, Will and Macon went inside. Macon Fallon looked appreciatively at the old house and its furnishings.

Seeing Fallon's gaze, Will spoke, "The house was originally built by my grandfather. The lumber was sawed from timber cleared to make room for crops. When Brandon and I came along, the house was added onto. We were lucky." He led Fallon over to a bar and raising a decanter of brandy, he got a nod from his new friend. Pouring two sniffers, he continued, "The war never made its way to this area, and most of the locals know nothing of war other than what they've read in the paper. That is unless, of course, they had family who was wounded or killed."

Macon Fallon nodded, knowing how difficult it was to imagine the hell of war, be it at sea or on land, unless you'd been there. He sensed that the man before him had been there. "Is that from the war?" he asked.

"Yes unfortunately. I was a surgeon in General Bragg's army at Chickamauga. The Yankees came around one of our flanks. Our field hospital was there and for a while we were between the two sides. Cannon balls cut huge holes in the surgical tent and then we were peppered with musket fire. My nurse was wounded by a Minie ball, and as I reached to save her a cannonball took off my hand. I'd be dead now, were it not for Shad's quick thinking." The men were silent for a while, each in their own thoughts.

The dogs started barking as Harvey Jordan, who was the local law, rode up. He was a tall gangly man with darkish hair under a flop hat. His face was bright and friendly with a ready smile. "I sent two Negroes in a wagon to get the body," he said. "I'll have to get everyone's statement, since it was a robbery."

"We understand," Will said.

"Did you recognize the sod?" Harvey asked.

"No, but he called Brandon preacher," Will answered.

"So he knew you all." It was a statement and not a question. "Well, I reckon that's one more soul that the county will have to bury," Harvey said.

"How much?" Fallon asked, speaking for the first time.

Harvey eyed the man, not used to anyone asking how much to bury a body. "There won't be any service that I can imagine. Seven dollars ought to see him planted proper."

Fallon reached into his pocket and took out some coins. He handed Harvey two five dollar gold pieces. "See if you can find a man of the cloth, and have him say a few words. Nobody should be buried without the words being said."

Will, thinking of Fallon as a sea captain, thought that he had probably read over many a soul whose body was committed to the deep.

***

AFTER A HEARTY BREAKFAST THE next morning Will took Fallon down to the stables to look at the family's horses. Fallon looked at the slave quarters as they walked.

"What are you going to do with those?" he asked.

"Nothing, the hands live in them."

"Hands?"

"Yes, you have to have hands to work a plantation. Without the hands, you couldn't grow a crop, especially cotton."

"Your slaves stayed?"

Lee smiled, "Yes. Brandon is a preacher, as you know. He holds church for the blacks every Saturday afternoon, so they trust him. He pledged to house and feed the people as it had been done when they were slaves. In addition, a percentage of the profits will be divided up among each family."

Fallon asked, "And they all stayed?"

"Most of them did, a few left. We also have a few sharecroppers. We furnish the land and seed, and they furnish everything else."

Fallon then pointed and asked, "What's that building?"

"It's a tobacco barn. We continue to grow tobacco in one field. It's a pretty good cash crop."

Fallon nodded, "It's a big plantation. I can see why it takes the two of you to run it."

"Not the two of us, just Brandon," Will replied, correcting Fallon. "He is the farmer. He has an overseer to help out, but not me. I was never interested. I was a surgeon. But now, I don't know." Will raised his wooden hand to punctuate his meaning. "Is there anything else you'd like to see?" he asked.

When Fallon said no, Lee smiled. "Well, I'm interested in your weapons."

"I knew that was coming," Fallon replied. "There's a table on the porch, let's go there."

Will nodded and called to a stable hand. "Mookie, go get Shad and tell him to meet me on the porch. I've something that I want him to see."

When Shad arrived he sat down next to Will and listened as Fallon discussed his pistols. "The one that I carry on my side is a Colt 1851 Navy. It's a .36 caliber Navy revolver. It's made exactly like the Colt .44 Walkers, only it's much lighter. It's not made to kill a horse like the .44's were made to do, but it's very deadly when firing at a man. It is made to carry in a belt holster, but I've modified mine so the holster has a slight tilt and is made for a cross draw. As I said, I find that more suitable for me and I'm a lot faster with it compared to the conventional carry method. The gun carries six rounds, cap and ball, but there's talk of a conversion coming so that the pistols will use metallic cartridges like the Henry rifles do. I don't have one, but I intend to buy one soon."

"The gun that I carry in my shoulder holster is a Colt model 1862 Navy. It is a modification of the Colt 1849 Pocket Navy that shot a .31 caliber ball."

"I've seen those," Will interjected.

"I'd be surprised if you hadn't, since Colt had sold over three hundred thousand at the time of his death. As you can see, the Pocket Navy is just slightly smaller than my other pistol. It has a shorter barrel. This one is 4 ½ inches long but you can order it in 5.5 or 6.5 inches, whichever length you prefer. It has only five shots but this is my emergency backup. If I need more than five shots, I'm already in trouble. Truth is, if one shot doesn't do it, you are usually dead anyway." Fallon stood, "If Shad would be so kind, I have my reloading supplies in a small bag in my room. If he'll go get it, we'll do a little target practice and I'll teach you how to load these pistols."

"There are plenty of bottles we can take down to the creek to shoot at," Shad volunteered, getting an evil look from Will and then a smile.

***

THE MEN PRACTICED FOR THE next two hours with the pistols. Will missed every time at first, but was soon hitting three bottles out of every six shots. He hit all six on his last round.

"I think we'll stop there," Fallon said. "I've just enough powder and ball left to load both pistols."

"My apologies," Will said, feeling guilty for shooting up his friend's supplies. "We have plenty of black powder but no .36 caliber balls or caps."

"I'll get more when we get to Mobile. I have a supplier there," Fallon responded.

"Good," Will answered. "Let's go get some refreshments."

The men played cards after being served some cool tea...plain tea. Will found that he could actually hold the cards he was dealt with the glove over his wooden hand. Fallon showed him how he could cut the cards one-handed and bet that Will, with the use of the wooden hand, could probably become very adept with the cards with a bit of practice.

"A good hand at poker can usually do very well for himself," Fallon said, "not here, but in Mobile, New Orleans, and even on the Mississippi River boats." He added, after a pause, "You can also lose your shirt, if not your life. You have to learn how to read the players as well as the cards."

Will thought of Fallon's words, as he made it to his room. *A good hand at poker can usually do very well for himself.* Back before the war, while in medical school, he'd sat in on a few poker games and without really trying to, he'd won more often than not. It was usually with a conversation about a lecture, or an upcoming test being discussed, so that his thoughts and conversations had not been on the cards. He'd also played with other surgeons during the war when time allowed. He could maybe make it playing cards. He would at least try it. It was better than looking for the bottom of a bottle every day.

CHAPTER THREE

THE NEXT YEAR WAS LIKE a whirlwind for Will and Shad. The two accompanied Macon Fallon and were so busy that Will rarely thought of his previous life as a noted surgeon. A few days after meeting Fallon and his visit to Eagle Trace, the three men met up with the British cotton agent, David Hayes, and went down the Flint River on a barge to Bainbridge, Georgia. They took a riverboat from there to Apalachicola, Florida. On the dock near Fallon's ship, *Falcon*, there were containers of wine, sugar, clothes, and rum to be loaded. The supplies were to be taken to Mobile, so they took passage on the *Falcon* as Fallon's guests, as they had become close friends. Both Will and Shad were excited to see Mobile.

The weather was fierce as they arrived in Mobile. The clouds were dark, the wind was howling, and the sea was choppy. The weather delayed their going ashore for twenty-four hours. Fallon, Will, and Mr. Hayes spent the extra time playing poker...a game that Will was becoming very good at. The next day the weather had cleared substantially. After taking care of the ship's business, Fallon took Will to a gun shop where he had done considerable business.

Fallon greeted the owner and introduced Will as Major Will Lee, a former officer under General Braxton Bragg. The shop owner shook hands with Lee, noticing the prosthetic right hand. "Thank you for your contribution to our glorious cause," the shop owner volunteered, making Will feel self-conscious.

Will looked over several guns, but when it was over he bought two pistols, the 1862 Colt Pocket Navy revolver and the latest edition of the Colt 1851 Navy. They were both a .36 caliber. He bought a shoulder holster and a holster for the larger Navy Pistol. He also bought one hundred caps and balls. Seeing Shad looking at a Fox 10 gauge shotgun, Will bought that as well, along with three boxes of shells.

Loaded down with the purchases, Fallon led the men up the street to a tavern called the Sailor's Rest. They rented two rooms on the second floor, and once again Fallon had introduced Will as Major Will Lee to the tavern owner. After they were up in their room, Will asked Fallon why he was using his previous military rank.

Fallon smiled and explained, "There's still a lot of sympathy for our Civil War veterans, especially with those who have suffered from the war. The use of major will open the door for you to be treated as a friend, which results in a greater discount when purchasing items. It will also open the door to the more elite citizens in the city."

"My title of doctor wouldn't have the same effect?" Will asked.

"Sadly no, there are a lot of doctors around but what did they contribute to the cause? You, Major, lost a hand. Your life has changed, take advantage of the courtesy being offered."

Will turned to Shad, "What do you think?"

Shad paused a second, obviously in thought. He finally said, "I like it. It's easier to say major than Mr. Lee. I forget to say Mister and I get evil looks from any white folks who may hear."

Will smiled, "I guess Major it will be."

Before they left the room, Shad took measurements for the shoulder holster and also the holster for the cross draw. He then found his way to a saddle and harness shop to get the supplies he needed to make the alterations.

The shoulder holster was ready the next morning, but Will's coat was too tight. Fallon then took Will to a tailor that he used for his uniforms. The tailor greeted Fallon as Captain Fallon. Will was introduced as Major Will Lee, a title that he was getting used to and liked. The tailor promised three new coats and five new shirts so that the sleeve over his prosthetic would fit much better.

Will was now short of funds, so Fallon took him to a gambling hall that evening, something that soon became a ritual. He frequented gambling halls, riverboats, and even a few private clubs. At the end of six months, Will was up four thousand dollars and was ready to go home. He had grown tired of the constant nightlife. During this time, Fallon had had to return to his ship, but leaving Will much more able to fend for himself.

In the months since Fallon had returned to sea, Will realized that by allowing his opponents to win a few hands, he'd established himself as a fair hand at the tables but not a card shark. He had run into one crooked riverboat gambler, but realizing what he was dealing with, he folded his hand and got out of the game. A couple of hands later, the gambler was caught dealing off the bottom. The man who called him out was a well-dressed man who looked to be sixty. On being called out, the gambler shoved the table into the older gentleman and went for his gun. He froze though, when the unmistakable sound of a hammer being cocked was like thunder in his ear. At the same time, he felt the cold steel of a gun barrel touch the side of his head. The gambler knew he was seconds from dying. The ship's captain was called and the gambler was thrown off the boat and the older gentleman introduced himself.

"I'm William Selleck. I own a ranch outside of Austin, Texas. If you are ever in the area, stop in."

Will thanked the gentleman but the only place that he had his mind set on visiting was Eagle Trace.

***

BRANDON WAS ECSTATIC TO SEE his brother looking so well. He didn't say anything about the gun on Will's side or the one under his coat that he felt when they hugged. Brandon shook Shad's hand, saying he knew it was Shad that had Will looking so fit. That night over a glass of wine...a rare glass for Brandon, they talked about all the latest news. Brandon was excited and could hardly contain himself when he told Will that he was taking a wife. The bride-to-be was Gabby, the young widow woman. Will had felt that his brother would ask for the lady's hand—Brandon had been infatuated with her since they had first met. The wedding was only three months away.

In regards to Eagle Trace, things were not as well. The war years had seen a substantial decrease in the plantation's profits. Brandon looked at Will and said, "Things are improving now, but the plantation is still fifteen hundred dollars behind in taxes. The only way I can see to keep from losing it all is to sell some of the land." It would take care of the immediate need but in the long run having fewer acres would mean less profit. It also meant that they'd have to let several hands go.

Will started to ask why he hadn't been told the plantation was in trouble. He then realized he'd lived two years in a drunken stupor.

His brother may have told him, or thought *what's the use*. He would remedy that now.

"No, we're not going to do either," Will said.

When Brandon started to protest that there was no other way, Will held up his hand to hush him. He then reached in his coat for his wallet and pulled out two thousand dollars.

"One thousand five hundred dollars for the taxes," he said. "And five hundred dollars as a wedding gift for you and Gabby."

Brandon sat there in disbelief. Draining the rest of the wine in one gulp, he tried to hide a tear in his eyes. "The Bible says have faith," Brandon said softly. Wiping away the remaining tears, he smiled. "I see your new profession has proved very profitable."

"Not always, but lately lady luck has smiled on us, now and again," Will admitted.

The following morning, Will had Caesar saddled. The stallion had not been ridden much during the time that Will was away. This morning he wanted to show his superiority as the dominant horse on the plantation. He bowed his back and bucked a bit when Will mounted, but a kick in his ribs and a slap with the reins calmed him down a bit. He still tried to nip at Brandon's red bay gelding. It was Brandon, this time, who gave the horse a slap across the nose with his bridle reins.

The men rode over to the general store for some cigars, after paying the taxes at the Starkville Courthouse. Brandon told Will, as they walked, that the local politicians were once again trying to move the county seat to another location. "Unless it's Wooten Station, I'd just as soon leave it where it is," Brandon said.

Suddenly they heard a galloping horse. It was Shad on a lathered horse, and Will felt his heart sink.

"Mr. Chandler wants you to come quick," Shad threw out. "Mizz. Jen and Mizz. Gabby has been taken."

"By whom?" Brandon asked, feeling like his stomach was in his mouth.

Shad replied, "One of the men was the brother of that man Captain Fallon killed."

CHAPTER FOUR

THE MEN, FORGETTING ABOUT THE cigars, pushed their horses to Chan Calhoun's home. Mrs. Calhoun's maid was there. She'd been present when the women were abducted. She'd cried until her eyes were very swollen. She was still hysterical when the men arrived.

"This poor girl has lost her wits," Chan swore.

"Give this girl a glass of brandy or sherry," Will recommended.

Shad, knowing where everything was located in the Calhoun house, ran to get the drink for the girl. Her eyes watered, after taking a large gulp of the fiery brandy, and she nearly choked. A moment later, she took another sip, and then another.

She was finally able to speak, "It was that nasty old Spencer Hastings. He said the preacher caused him to lose his brother, so the preacher was gonna find out what it's like to lose somebody. He hadn't been after Mizz. Jen, but said that he'd keep her as a hostage and to show Mr. Chandler he wasn't so high and mighty. He let me go but said not to follow or he'd kill both of the women."

Will snorted and said, "They'll be killed anyway." He didn't add after they'd been used up.

"No sir," Bess, the maid, replied. "He said that he'd send word and for ten thousand dollars Mizz. Jen would be set free."

Will asked, "Which way did they head out?"

"Toward Albany, sir, or in that general direction," the maid replied.

"Did he ask for ransom for Gabby?" Brandon asked. The girl shook her head no.

"They don't know that I'm here, so that's good," Will said. "Shad, ride Caesar back to the house and get Buck and Blue." They were Will's bloodhound and bulldog. "Bring them back in a wagon and bring me that roan gelding." He paused for a moment and then added, "Bring your shotgun and a box of shells."

Shad smiled, "Yes, sir, Major." Brandon and Chan looked up at the term major but Will ignored them.

He turned to Bess, "Can you take me back to the last spot that you saw them?"

"Yes sir, I think I can."

"Good girl." Will turned then to Brandon and Chan, "I don't expect you'll get any ransom note or demands. I think that was a ploy to keep you off their trail. If you do get a note, stall...stall as long as you can. Give me something of Jen's so that Buck can trail her."

Chan asked, "Think he can?"

Will smiled, "That's what bloodhounds do. Slaves feared having a bloodhound on a trail. Blue, he's just hell on somebody if they try to hurt me. We'll get the women back so don't you worry."

"I'll worry, but I feel better knowing that you are going after them," Chan said.

I wish I did, Will thought, but he kept it to himself. He was not feeling good about finding the rogues.

***

WILL AND SHAD FOLLOWED BUCK for two days as he trailed the group. Will was disappointed after the first day, and still no sight of their prey. Buck, however, still seemed to be following the scent well and the first night he had to be restrained to keep from going on without Will and Shad.

Shad had been thoughtful enough to have a bundle of food and coffee put together with a frying pan, coffee pot, two metal plates and cups with forks. When he got ready to fry some bacon, he used his own pocket knife. Their supper consisted of strong black coffee, bacon, and cornbread.

The trail, by the end of the second day, looked fresher. There was also an attempt by one of the women to leave plain signs. Food crumbs, part of a scarf, and once a pink hair bow. *Did they know that someone was coming after them?*

Will and Shad, that second night, set up camp where Hasting and his men had camped. After eating that night and washing the cookware in a small creek, Will and Shad pulled back. They moved back far enough so as not to disturb anything or anyone else from using the creek for water.

Buck and Blue both stood up about two a.m., with Blue giving a low, deep-throated growl. Will and Shad were instantly up. Will put his hand over the dog's mouth and Shad went to the horse and mules. The shadow of a man could be seen after a few minutes. He seemed uneasy about the camp but was determined to get down to the water. The bank and brush was too high and thick for at least a mile in any direction, so this was the only spot to get water.

Was he alone, Will wondered? *Where was his horse? Did he have a horse? Was somebody holding the horses until the area could be scouted* out? Will finally made up his mind, "If you are a friend, come in. If not, slap leather." His voice had been in a normal conversational tone. He had not expected the man to actually reach for a gun... but he did.

The man drew, fired and rolled, but when he came up, Will did as he'd been taught and put a slug dead center of the man's chest. Will waited several minutes before moving from behind a tree. The man had cried out and moaned the entire time.

Buck and Blue were struggling to get loose. Shad came over with a rope and tied the two dogs, and then with his shotgun in hand, he said, "Go ahead and check the man if you want, Major. I have this shotgun ready."

When Will was close enough, he recognized the man as a loafer who hung around the tavern in Wooten Station. Will, kneeling down next to the man could see that he didn't have long. Blood oozed from a hole dead center of the man's chest. "Why did you draw?" Will asked.

"I figured you were after us."

"Us who?" Will replied, faking ignorance.

"Me, Hastings and Meadows."

"Why would we be after you?"

"It was us that took the women."

"What women and why did you take them?"

"For sport and money Hastings said. Only there ain't going to be no money."

"Why'd you leave the others?" Will asked.

The man coughed and blood came from his mouth. His eyes looked glassy. Will knew the man only had a few minutes to live at best.

"Get me a canteen," Will called to Shad.

The man tried to spit, with the bloody sputum running down the side of his mouth. He then tried to talk again. "Things didn't work out with two women and three men. I fought Meadows, and when I had him down Hastings kicked me off him. I saw the way things were and lit out."

"How far ahead are they?"

The man tried to sit up and take the canteen that Shad offered, but he spit up more blood and collapsed again. Will thought that he'd spoken his last word when he said, "Three hours maybe, but don't worry. They gonna enjoy the women a spell before they move on." He coughed up more blood and called out a name that neither Will nor Shad could understand. The man died then.

Will handed the man's pistol to Shad for safekeeping. They then pulled the man away from the creek and piled what rocks they could over the body. The one thing they hadn't brought with them was a shovel.

Will took his timepiece out and could see that it was three a.m. "Let's load up and pull out, Shad. I couldn't go back to sleep now anyway."

Shad nodded and hitched up the mules while Will went looking for the man's horse; which was just past the camp and tied to a pine tree. Shad heard a 'dammit' and saw Will looking disgusted when he walked to the back of the wagon.

"Idiot had no better sense than to tie the reins to a pine tree. Now there's sap on the reins," Will said.

Shad smiled and then added, "And on the major's hands."

Will rubbed his hands in mud by the creek and then wiped them on a piece of burlap. That helped some but did not get rid of all the sticky sap.

They rode on down the trail for about two hours. Buck had bayed a few times so Will knew that they were getting close. He fashioned a muzzle of sorts and put it on the bloodhound. He then put both dogs in the wagon. Blue was whining but stopped when Will scolded him.

"We are near Cuthbert," Shad whispered. "I've been hunting over here with Mr. James a while back." Will's dad loved to hunt and a friend had invited him to a fox hunt in Cuthbert.

They had only gone a few more miles when they topped a rise and saw the red coals of a campfire in the distance.

"That's got to be them," Shad whispered.

"My thoughts as well," Will replied. "Let's get the rig down in the valley and go the rest of the way on foot."

It was just before dawn when Will and Shad drew near the fire. The two men were on ground blankets. A pistol was near one man's hand and a musket was near the other man. Jen was tied to a tree but it took a minute to locate Gabby. She was tied, hand and foot, with a rope tied to her and the hand of one of the men. If things turned bad she could be caught in the crossfire. Will had Shad crawl up to Jen. She'd recognize Shad but he wasn't sure that Gabby would.

Will crawled toward Gabby. The sound of him crawling, or some other sense, woke her up. He had seen the empty whiskey bottles near the fire and hoped the alcohol would cause the men to sleep much deeper than Gabby. Seeing the look of fright on the girl's face, Will put his fingers to his lips and continued crawling. Using his good hand, he passed the knife to Gabby. He looked down to take the thong off of his pistol and when he looked up, he was staring into the business end of a Colt Walker.

The man was sweaty, unshaven, and smelled to high heaven. His breath reeked of cheap whiskey and chewing tobacco. He'd either heard or sensed Will approaching, or Gabby had awakened him reaching for the knife or cutting her bonds. Will thought he was doomed either way when the man cocked the Walker and gave an evil grin.

Without thinking, Will drew his pistol with his good hand and shoved the wooden hand into the barrel of the rogue's gun. The sound of two guns firing as one broke the stillness of the night. Splinters went everywhere as the Walker fired into the wooden hand. Will didn't have time to aim; he just pointed his gun at the man's face and pulled the trigger. A hole appeared between the man's eyes and his nose as he fell back.

The other kidnapper, meanwhile, rose up and swung his musket around to fire. Before he could pull the trigger, Shad cut loose with the Fox and nine double-aught buck shots penetrated his chest and upper body. Both rogues were dead in a matter of seconds.

The women had been bruised and battered but neither of them had been molested. Gabby looked at Will and said, "It was to have happened tonight. They bragged about taking us tonight, but the men drank too much and were far too drunk, so we were both dreading the morning."

"I'm glad that we got here in time," Will said. He had more that he wanted to say but couldn't find the words. The look of the women and the shape of their clothes was testament enough for what they had been through.

When Shad returned with the wagon and dogs, Will had him help drag the bodies over near a deep wash. "Do we go into Cuthbert and report this," Shad asked.

Will Lee paused and looked at the women and then Shad, "No, the varmints will take care of the bodies and the women don't need to be put through any more." What Will didn't say was that he didn't want to report Shad's part in the shooting. Regardless of how right the situation was, a black man killing a white man would cause unrest in the community. He'd have to speak to the women about that. Gathering up the men's weapons, two Walker Colts and the musket, they started the trip home.

***

THE TRIP HOME WENT FASTER as they were not trying to follow a trail. Once home, there was a jubilant reunion. They'd met a neighbor's son on the way back and Will had given the boy a dollar to ride to the Calhoun home and notify Mr. Chandler that the women were safe and to meet them at Eagle Trace. As the group greeted each other warmly, Gabby told how she'd awakened from her sleep and saw Will crawling towards her. "It was like he was a ghost. In his uniform, I thought it's a ghost...a gray ghost."

CHAPTER FIVE

T HE NEXT THREE MONTHS WENT very quickly. Chan Calhoun had a mare that they'd bred to Caesar. She was now due to foal. Brandon and Gabby had wed and went to Charleston to meet Gabby's relatives and for her family to meet Brandon. They both had tried to get Will to accompany them. Will smiled and said, "Haven't you ever heard that two's plenty on a honeymoon."

Later when she was sure no one would hear, Gabby said to Will, "I do wish you would come along. I'm...I'm not sure how to say this. I love Brand. I love him dearly, but I feel safe with you around."

Will smiled, "Brand, as you call him, may not show it outwardly, but my brother can be holy hell..." He paused as it came to mind of Brandon's calling as a minister. "Let me rephrase that. Brother Brandon can be a terror when pushed to it. I can't count the times that he came to my aid when my mouth got me in trouble." Will paused again, a smile on his lips, "If ever asked, I'll deny it; but when we were growing up I was afraid to tangle with him."

Gabby was smiling now, "I believe that he can give an account of himself. I've seen...uh...I mean I've felt his muscles when he's hugged me."

A little smile creased Will's face, "Don't try to lie, Gabby, the cat's out of the bag." She looked flustered for a minute and then smiled back.

Brandon hearing them laugh walked into the parlor. "What's so funny?" he asked. The two looked at Brandon, hushed and then started laughing again. They'd managed to stop when he asked again, "Well, what's so funny?"

Will had always been quick, so he said, "Waking Gabby while crawling toward her with a wooden hand and a knife between my teeth."

Brandon smiled now, "I bet that was funny." As Brandon and Gabby started walking out of the room, she turned her head and mouthed the word "liar".

✸✸✸

SHAD HAD CARVED WILL A new hand, adding a few improvements over the old hand. He then went to work on two more hands, each in a different position. One was made to resemble a fist. He measured and remeasured it. "It occurred to me that you may be called upon to fight. If it's a planned thing, this would be a definite asset."

"But not necessarily fair," Will said.

"Major, the way I figure it, if a man picks a fist fight with a one-handed man, he deserves what he gets."

The second hand took the longest to get right. Shad said that he was making the hand to hold some special writing quills he was also making. What he didn't say was when he was finished, it would also hold a surgeon's scalpel. Shad rode Caesar into Wooten Station and bought extra pieces of leather, some leather string, and a leather softener...a softener that he had special ordered. He didn't want

Will's hand smelling like saddle soap and the leather had to be kept soft.

One of the workers met Shad as he returned, telling him of an oak that had been struck by lightning down close to the creek. Seeing how he'd already used the previous blocks he'd cut and let dry, this was a huge find. They cut the tree down and trimmed off the branches. It left a trunk about eight feet long and about ten inches around. Shad cut off two blocks, each twelve inches long, and put them in his cabin. The remainder he had put across the trusses in the barn to dry. *Hopefully, they won't be needed,* Shad thought, *but with the major who knew.*

***

WILL HAD JUST RETURNED FROM the Calhoun's. The colt had been born and looked like a miniature Caesar. Galloping down the lane was Harvey Jordan's jailer, Pinky.

"I'm glad I caught you before you went to bed, Mr. Lee. The sheriff asks if you could come quickly, sir. There's been a killin' and likely to be more."

Will mounted Caesar and followed the jailer. Pinky was riding a mule that had the poor man bouncing up and down. While Will cringed with every bounce and jolt, Pinky rode on indifferently, seemingly oblivious to it.

Will could see as they neared the town that Moore's Tavern was well lit. At one end of the tavern was a barber shop but the windows to the shop were black. A crowd of people were gathered around on the tavern porch, and standing just outside and to one side of the door was Harvey.

"I'm glad that you could come, Major."

Damn, Will thought, *is everyone calling me that now.* Harvey has known me since I was a teenager. Handing Caesar's reins to Pinky, Will walked over to the sheriff. "What's going on?" he asked.

"That blasted billiard table has got a man killed. I told Moore when he put it in that it would cause trouble, and now it has. Comer and Eugene got into an argument over a game. The next thang you know, Comer has done shot Eugene. He's still laying thar. The sawdust is soaking up his blood."

"I see," Will said. "Comer won't come out?"

"No, he just sits thar on the table. Sez he'll kill anybody that comes in, and that he done kilt Eugene and you only hang once, no matter how many you kill."

Will digested this and asked, "How can I help you, Harvey?"

"If you peek around the door, you can see the window on the other side is open. If you will go around thar, you can put a bead on Comer. You keep him covered and I'll go in unarmed and see if he will give up without somebody else getting killed."

"Why'd you pick me?" Will asked. "Surely, there are plenty of men closer than me."

"Not what shoots like you do, son. I need a man with a good eye and not afraid to pull the trigger if need be."

Will nodded but wondered who'd been talking. He'd killed two men rightly enough, but that was to have been a secret. Will made his way to the opposite side and the open window of the tavern. He waved to Pinky who, in turn, waved to the sheriff.

Will stood to the side of the window until he heard Harvey call out, "Comer...it's me, Harvey Jordan. We need to talk."

"No, stay out."

"Comer, you know that I can't do that. Look, we're friends. I've et buttermilk and cornbread plenty of times, sitting on your porch. I'm unarmed now, so I'm coming in."

Will had to give it to the old lawman, he had a way with his words. Looking, Will could see that Harvey was filling the doorway entrance and that he wasn't dealing with a sober man. An empty bottle was on the table and Comer had another bottle in his hand taking a swig. He had his musket in the other hand, with the hammer cocked. *Had Comer reloaded it?* Will was sure that he had.

Harvey took another step in the room. He continued to make small talk with Comer but to no obvious effect.

Comer, turning up the bottle, drained the last of the whiskey. "Harvey, you got one minute to make peace with your maker," Comer shouted. "I done kilt one friend, I might as well make it two."

Harvey replied, "That's the whiskey talking, Comer."

"Don't matter who's talking, it's this gun what's doing the killing." Comer saying that lifted the musket.

"Don't, Comer," Will shouted. "I have you covered. Put the gun down or you're dead before you can pull the trigger."

Comer turned his head toward the window, and when he did, Harvey took a step to the side so that he'd be harder for Comer to shoot at. "Glory be," Comer snarled. "Our pistolero major." Saying that, Comer swung his gun around and pulled the trigger, tearing splinters from the window frame.

Will jerked to one side, but true to his word a .36 caliber ball entered Comer's head. It had been a close call still. *Way too close,* Will thought.

"You all right, Harvey?"

"Yeah! You?"

● ● ●

WILL RODE HOME, LETTING CAESAR slowly pick his way down the trail. The horse seemed to pick up on his rider's mood. *I need a drink,* Will thought, but was glad that one wasn't available. The way that he felt right now, he'd drink the whole damn bottle. He didn't want to slide down that slope again. The thought kept coming to his mind, *I have killed again.* His first victims were doing his family harm and he'd acted quickly, decisively, and felt no remorse. But now, he'd killed Comer, a man he'd known most of his life. *Have I been too quick to shoot?* It had been a reaction...a lightning fast reaction. Had he been slower on the trigger, maybe Harvey and some men could have subdued Comer. Now he'd never know. *Damn it, why had Harvey called me?* Had his ability with a gun overshadowed his once being a surgeon? He had now taken several lives. He'd once made an oath to protect life, and now here he was taking life. *Is this to be my destiny?* As he drew up and dismounted at the stable, he thought, *at least I saved Harvey from getting his head blown off, that's what I will dwell on.*

For days, the talk around Wooten Station was all about the shooting. It was all wrong, but Harvey was the only eyewitness, so he could tell it like he wanted to. He had said that Major Lee stood there cool as could be and didn't fire until Comer fired at him. It was all true, but then Harvey added, 'If Major Lee hadn't fired, Comer would have likely turned and shot him. *With what,* Will thought. He only had the one gun that Will could remember. But Will didn't contradict the old lawman. Opinions might change if people were told differently.

When Chan and Jen had Will over for dinner, Chan spoke to his friend, "Will, you have saved my Jen and we are grateful. You saved Harvey and he's certainly grateful. But, my friend, you are creating a reputation for yourself as a shootist. As much as we would miss you, I think you need to consider heading west for a while. Let the talk of these shootings die down. I don't want you or your family becoming a target of some relative of the men you've killed."

CHAPTER SIX

THE SOUND OF THE WHISTLE from the riverboat was blasting away. Shad had just put Will's things in his stateroom, and after a thought he stood the double barrel shotgun in the corner behind the door. They had left Eagle Trace a week after Brandon and Gabby had returned from their honeymoon. It had been a sad good-bye but the newlyweds needed time to themselves.

They went to Mobile first, thinking that they might by chance encounter Macon Fallon, but he was at sea. After a few nights in Mobile, where Will won five hundred dollars, they traveled to New Orleans. Will became friends...close friends, with a lady who owned a gambling house. Margaret, Marge to her friends, had once been a beautiful woman. She did not look bad now, but her hair was so white, it obviously came out of a bottle. Crow's feet were starting to develop at the corners of her eyes. She wore makeup to hide them and other wrinkles that were starting to develop. Yes, too many nights in a smoked filled gambling house and bar had caused her to age beyond her years. Will's dexterity with the cards for a one-handed man was what had first caught her attention. She soon learned that he was not some tin horn card shark. He actually won with skill and the knowledge of how the men around him played, exploiting their mannerisms and facial expressions in different situations. How they bid and when they tended to bluff, but more importantly how their eyes moved when they had a winning hand. In short, Major Will Lee knew how to read men, and so did Marge. She never complained about Shad standing in a corner. That was Lee's protection—a man who watched over his blind side. Had she protested, Lee would have moved to another gambling house. After a few days, she invited Lee to move into an empty room upstairs. It had two beds and Shad could stay there as well. It was next to her room, with an adjoining door. She knew that he would not stay long. His kind never did, but she intended to make the most of their time together.

Will had been in New Orleans for a month. He'd made money and had sent some home to be banked and used if the plantation ran short. It was now time to move. His skill was becoming known and fewer people wanted to play with him. As he and Shad set out for a walk down Market Street, Will had a taste for a muffuletta—a loaf of sesame bread split and filled with layers of marinated olive salad, salami, ham, Swiss cheese, provolone and mortadella. They ended up at a coffee and sandwich shop that Will liked, run by a local Italian. Finishing their sandwich and beer, Will and Shad decided to walk off some of their lunch. As he left the sandwich shop, Will, by chance, happened upon Mr. William Selleck, the rancher from Austin.

Mr. Selleck, finding that Will had no set plans, persuaded him to accompany him on a trip to Austin. "See Austin, see Texas, you'll never want to go home," Selleck bragged. Will finally agreed to go.

He went and packed his things and said good-bye to Marge as she tried to hold back her tears. She would miss Major Will Lee, she would miss him a lot.

The steamship, *Texas Ranger*, would take them to Galveston, where Selleck had business. They would then go overland to Austin. At night, on board the steamship, they could try their luck at the tables. Will won a couple hundred dollars at the tables, in mostly low stake games between men who were obviously well acquainted, if not actual friends. One of the men at the table called Selleck 'general'. Will asked about the rank later.

Selleck smiled, "I was in charge of a group of men organized to deal with the scum and riff-raff that eventually comes during a war. I really never commanded anything or held any official rank."

Will smiled and said, "I like the term. It makes me feel better being called major."

Selleck laughed, "Well, in your case, at least it's not a fake title."

Will was somewhat amazed when they reached Galveston. The trip had only taken thirty-three hours and when they arrived, Will had only slept in his stateroom once.

The wharf at Galveston was in sad shape. "The Civil War caused that," Selleck volunteered, seeing Will's gaze upon the sorry state of repairs the wharf represented.

Bales of cotton still filled the wharf, leaving only a small path for passengers to walk. Hearing a whistle, Will looked to Selleck.

"Galveston has a railroad?"

"A short one, Major. It runs from Galveston to Houston."

Will shook his head, suitably impressed as a porter walked up with Selleck's bags. Shad and Will managed to carry their bags to the end of the wharf, where they enlisted a Negro boy with a wheelbarrow. They walked to the Tremont Hotel, wishing that they'd taken a carriage.

Selleck was well known there and in minutes two rooms were provided. There were no suites available. Since blacks were not allowed in the normal guest rooms, the clerk put Shad up in a room in back of the hotel, close to the kitchen.

Selleck was introduced to a man by the name of James Robinson at dinner that evening. He owned a construction company and he had plans for rebuilding the wharf.

Will found Shad after dinner, and the two of them walked around Galveston. Hearing a commotion behind them, Will and Shad turned. Two men, obviously drunk, had crashed out of a saloon. The fight turned deadly then. The bigger man knocked a much smaller man...really a kid...off the plank sidewalk and into the muddy street.

"I've had enough of your bullying, Swede," the kid, hurt and angered, shouted at the big man.

Swede turned and found himself staring down the barrel of the kid's Colt. Before Swede could react, the sound of the gun echoed in the night. Swede fell face down on the planks.

The kid then looked at Will and Shad, "He'll pester me no more." He holstered his gun and walked back into the saloon.

An onlooker shook his head, "Swede should've known better than to pick on the Brazos kid. He may be small but that Colt makes him as 'pizzon' as a rattlesnake."

"Not a man that I'd want to anger," Will volunteered.

"No, me either," Shad admitted. "Did you see how quick he drew that pistol?"

Will nodded his head in the affirmative. Deciding that they'd seen enough, the two men went back to the hotel.

CHAPTER SEVEN

HE STAGECOACH RIDE TO AUSTIN had not been comfortable.
They stopped every fifteen to thirty miles, depending on
the terrain, and ate hurried meals at a couple of the stops. At
night, they had layovers. One stop was nothing more than bunk
beds hastily put together. The next night though, they stayed in a
handsome two-story white house.

Supper that night was venison, beans, potatoes, hot biscuits
and coffee. Milk was also offered. In one corner was a small bar
with beer and a limited variety of whiskey.

The beds were real feather beds and two rooms had been set
aside for the ladies. A bath could be had for the asking and a dollar.

They made Austin the next evening. It had been a hard trip since
arriving in Galveston. However, Selleck looked no worse for wear.
That evening they stayed in the Bullock Hotel. After the evening
meal, Selleck hired a rig to show off his Capitol.

Driving down Congress Avenue, Selleck pointed out how wide
the street was running up to the Capitol. They then stopped at the
Old Bakery to buy a bag each of donuts and apple fritters. Selleck

then had the driver take them by Scholz Garten. It had just been opened that year by a German but from the crowd Will figured it would be around a while.

An older black man was at the livery stable a little after daylight the next day. "Morning, Alan," Selleck greeted the hostler. "Get my horse out, if you will, and also get me two pack mules and two horses for my friends."

"They are going with you, Mr. William?" Alan asked.

"That they are. We are going to leave our bags here and go over to Mattie's for breakfast."

Mattie's was a medium sized café with eight round tables and stools at the counter. The breakfast menu was written on a chalkboard and consisted of eggs, fried potatoes, biscuits and gravy, flat cakes and syrup. You had a choice of beef, bacon, ham, or sausage for meat. At the bottom of the menu, it listed oatmeal for those toothless customers. You could have coffee, tea, or milk to drink. Bread was listed as biscuits, leftover cornbread or white bread. When the meal was finished, Will thought, *maybe a nap is more in order than a saddle,* but being game he climbed astride a big bay gelding.

Selleck began talking about his ranch, the Lazy S, once they were on the trail. "The ranch lies between the Colorado and the Brazos Rivers, and consists of five hundred thousand acres, or nearly eight hundred square miles. There's plenty of water compared to the dry west Texas. We run cattle, mostly longhorns, but I'm beginning to experiment with a few Herefords."

The three men stopped by a creek at noon to water their horses and heat up a pot of coffee. While enjoying their coffee, Selleck continued to talk about all it took to keep a cattle ranch going, especially a large one like the Lazy S. He had just dumped the coffee grounds when they heard the thunder of hooves.

Selleck quickly climbed on his horse and peered out. He took his pistol out after a moment and fired three shots. The riders drew up, spotted Selleck waving his hat and recognizing their boss, they hurried over.

"We've got rustlers," the leader said. "They took over a hundred head. We have been on their trail since daybreak."

Selleck called to a hand in the group, "Luke, take my guests on to the ranch."

Will volunteered, before Selleck could speak anymore, "If it's all the same, I'd just as soon ride with you."

"It will be a hard ride," Selleck advised.

"Don't worry about my hand," Will said. He then looked at Shad, "You want to ride or go to the ranch?"

"I'll ride," Shad volunteered.

Selleck nodded and said, "Hobble the pack animals, Luke, and then try to catch up."

"Yes sir."

The group then bounded off with the big man, who'd spoken to Selleck, in the lead. The horses were lathered up and started to blow when the men slowed up. A dead cow was on the trail. Will looked at Shad, who raised his eyebrows; as the big man got down to check the cow. Will thought that he was a horseman, but what he was used to was like a Sunday walk compared to what they were doing now.

"Not more than an hour I'd say, Mr. Selleck," the big man reported.

Selleck nodded and then threw out, "They'll have to slow down now. Otherwise, they'll lose too many."

"There's a creek about a mile further," the big man said. "We can water the horses there." The men rode off again at a gallop.

Could Caesar stand up to this type of hard riding? Will wondered. He was definitely a prize around Lee County, Georgia but Will seriously doubted that he could stand up to these cow horses.

The men climbed down at the creek, loosened the cinches on their horses and let them drink a bit before pulling them back. A couple of men were using a wet handkerchief to wipe out the horses' nostrils.

Will saw something then that went against all of his medical training. The men were drinking from the creek right where the horses had watered. One of the men was now filling his canteen from the creek.

Shad looked at the rough cowhands and spoke to Will, "Ain't much like home is it, Major?"

Selleck laughed hearing this, "I've drank in much worse."

The big man walked over, "You ready, boss?"

"Yes...ah Ben, I want you to meet Major Will Lee. He's the gentleman who saved my life."

"Pleased to meet you, Major."

Will then said, "This is Shad. We grew up together back in Georgia."

Ben shook Shad's hand, and turned to Selleck, "We better ride."

The cinches were tightened, Shad doing Will's horse and then his own. They splashed across the creek and were galloping up a rise when Ben held up his hand and the riders pulled up. He looked at Selleck and said, "Listen." It took Will a moment to realize what Ben's experienced ear had picked up...cattle lowing.

"They can't be far," Ben said.

The sun was low and it wouldn't be long until sundown. The rustlers had probably decided to rest. They'd been at it since some time last night or early this morning.

"We better go slowly from here on," Ben said.

Selleck was the owner, but it was clear to Will that it was the big, hard-looking foreman who ran things...the cattle aspect anyway. He was tall, rawboned, not an ounce of fat on the man. His eyes were a cold, pale blue that seemed to look right through you. When he'd shaken hands with Will, they were strong...rough and strong. But there was nothing rough about the walnut grips on his Colts. They were shiny and smooth, even in the dying light.

Ben called out several names and ordered two men to the left flank and two to the right. They started moving out slowly. They crossed the open space and as they started up a rise the cattle's lowing grew much louder. Before them was another rise.

"They're probably over that rise," Ben said, his voice low like the sound would carry over the cattle lowing.

"They didn't let the cattle water long," Selleck said. "Those cows are thirsty."

"Probably thought they'd drink all they wanted once they get to Benteens."

Selleck snorted, "We need to wipe that place off the map. It's nothing but a hangout for outlaws and rustlers."

Topping the rise on their hands and knees, they saw the rustlers. Their horses were tied to a rope strung between two trees. Saddles were on the ground around a campfire and coffee had been put on. Going back down the rise, Ben told the riders what they'd found. The flankers had come back in and gathered with the rest.

Ben turned to his boss and asked, "How do you want to handle it, Mr. Selleck?"

"I think that we'll circle the camp. Mingo," he spoke to a rider who appeared to be an Indian, or maybe Indian and Mexican mix. "Did you see any nightriders or lookouts?"

"No Señor, no one was with the herd. I didn't see a lookout."

Selleck nodded, "Ben, send a few men to cover the horses. Let two or three men go to the other side of the camp and we'll make our way down from here."

Ben spoke up then, "Ain't any of those boys looking to stretch a rope, so they'll come up shooting. Be ready, but don't shoot one of our men." The riders mumbled their understanding.

Selleck gave the men time to move out, and then spoke to Will, "Major, there's going to be shooting going on..."

Will broke him off in mid-sentence, "We've come this far, we'll go on."

Selleck slapped him on the shoulder, "I figured that but had to mention it." He turned, without waiting for a reply, and started toward the rustler's camp.

It was full dusk when they neared the camp. The rustlers were drinking coffee and complaining about the hard ride. One of the men spoke to another; "He'll hush complaining once he get his cut."

Selleck spoke out, "There isn't going to be any cut."

Startled, the rustlers went for their guns, but having been staring into the fire, their vision was not focused. Finally, one of the rustlers threw a shot and all hell broke loose. For the next forty-five seconds to a minute, the constant ring of guns firing and streaks of flames from the pistols' barrels lit up the early evening. One man jumped up to run for it, but Selleck moved to cut him off. A pistol fired and Selleck went down, grabbing his leg. The rustler was past Selleck now. Will turned and, even in the bad light, he could make out his man. Will's Navy Colt barked and the man staggered and then fell.

Will turned again and suddenly it dawned on him that the firing had stopped. A couple of Selleck's riders were checking the downed rustlers. Ben had been right. They were a desperate lot once they'd been caught.

"Pity we ain't got one to hang," Luke said. "It would send a message to the thieving devils."

"String one up anyway," Mingo recommended.

They built the fire up and Will looked at Selleck. He said, feeling on the man's leg, "It didn't hit the bone, thank goodness, but the bullet is still in there. I can feel it when I run my hand down the back of your thigh."

Selleck nodded and said, "Ben, have some of the boys drift the cattle back to the water, and then cut the damn bullet out." The thirsty cows were noisier now than before the shooting.

Luke came back over to Will, "Where'd you aim at when you shot that rustler, Major?"

"Does it matter?"

"It does to me."

"I didn't want a wounded man to get away in the dark, so I shot him in the head."

"You sure as the devil did," Luke squawked. "A running man, near dark and you nailed him. It makes me want to be sure of my manners around you, sir."

Ben said, "Now that you've embarrassed the boss's guest, Luke, suppose you go with the boys drifting the cows back to water."

As Luke walked off, he was telling a friend that he didn't see any holes in the man until his match went out. "I thought he might be faking it until I lit another match. I saw his head then."

The voices faded out as they carried Selleck over to the fire. Ben cut his pants leg and then set his knife in the edge of the fire.

"What are you doing?" Will asked.

"I'm going to cut out that bullet."

"Mr. Selleck needs a doctor."

Before Ben could speak, Selleck spoke up, "It's a day's ride to town and a day's ride back. Mortification would set in before they got back." Selleck held up his hand to Will, "It's the way we do things out here, Major."

CHAPTER EIGHT

MAJOR WILL LEE STOOD THERE in the dark, looking down at his friend. A friend who'd likely die if cut on like they planned. He would surely stand a chance of losing the leg which might then kill him. Could he do it? Could he take out the bullet with his left hand? He did everything else with it. He could certainly shoot with it.

It was almost as if Shad was reading his mind, "You couldn't do any worse."

Will shook his head, "Get my box out of the saddle bag, Shad." Turning to Selleck, he said, "Before this," holding up the wooden hand, "I was a surgeon. I'll remove the bullet." Ben made to protest but closed his mouth. Will then said, "Anybody have any whiskey?"

"Si," Mingo said, and went to get his bottle.

"Pour out that coffee and somebody put on some water to boil." Will looked around at the rough cowhands looking at him, and not a one spoke.

"Shad, bring me that new white shirt," Will called out. It would be the cleanest thing he could use as a dressing. He had Shad tear the shirt up into several rags when he returned with it.

Selleck drank down most of the whiskey while Will cleaned the blood away from the wound. He then surprised everyone when he poured some of the whiskey in the wound, causing Selleck to grimace.

"Shad, you'll have to help." Will had the men build the fire up for more light, even though it made him sweat. There were no lanterns to use. "We're ready," Will said, speaking to Selleck. He then had a few of the hands get ready to hold their boss down. "Ben, take this bottle and splash a bit on our hands. It's said that it will help keep down infection. Let's do this."

With Selleck being held down by the hands, Will cut across the top of the bullet. He then applied pressure and the bullet popped through the skin. It was intact. "Thank God," Will said, and tossed the bullet in a pan. "Keep pressure here for a moment, Shad." He then took a probe and passed it through the wound, causing Selleck to squirm and groan.

A small bit of cloth was on the end of the probe. "That's what I was worried about," Will said. He took a strip of the shirt and wet it with whiskey and then passed it through the wound back to front. There was more cloth from the pants leg on it. Turning Selleck slightly, he matched the patch to the hole in the britches. "Damn, there's more," he swore.

This time he poured half of the whiskey that was left, in the back side of the wound and passed another strip of white shirt through. The rest of the cloth came out. Sighing, Will took the bottle of whiskey and poured the rest through the wound. Will stood up after bandaging the leg, "It's in God's hand now."

"Thank you, Major," Ben, the foreman said, gripping Will's shoulder. "I've never seen a better job."

Will smiled and sat down. *It's another hurdle I've overcome*, he thought.

Ben called to a man. "Lefty! Go back to the ranch and get a wagon. Put a mattress, some blankets, some food and water in it, and bring back another bottle of whiskey. Ride now, pronto." He then spoke to the man, Mingo, "Check those rustlers' saddlebags. There's bound to be at least one bottle of whiskey in them."

Good idea, I need a drink; Will thought, as he settled back on a saddle next to Selleck.

✸✸✸

WILL SAT UNDER A LIVE oak tree. He was enjoying a sandwich and a glass of cool apple cider. He'd come out to relax in the warm afternoon sun. It had been nearly a month since a hand had come from the ranch with a spring wagon to take Mr. Selleck home. A girl, or woman he should say, had been driving the wagon. The way she handled the reins and controlled the two horses told Will she was not a novice...she could drive. She had long brownish hair and her body was such that even at the distance he'd first seen her, she would never be mistaken as a man. Even in men's clothes she was a woman...unmistakably a woman! Selleck had called her Lainie. She was not his daughter, though she could have been. She was not his wife, nor his mistress. She was mistress of the household. Will found out later that her name was Lainie Stanton. Regardless of her title, she had a special loving relationship with Selleck. She nursed and fussed over Selleck like a daughter would.

The ranch house had been built when the threats of Indians and marauders were a big concern. The adobe walls were over two feet thick, which for some reason unknown to Will helped the house stay warm at night and cool during the day. The ranch house was painted white, with only the protruding beams a brown color. The bunkhouse was of similar construction, with only the barn being made of wood.

Will turned as he heard a door open to see Selleck walk out onto the veranda. He was using the crutches that Shad had made. Lainie followed with two glasses, bourbon for Selleck and wine for herself.

"What type of wine is that?" Will asked, picking up the scent on a slight breeze.

"It's a Mexican type of wine made with fruits. One of our men, Juan Montoya, is quite adept at making it. He uses grapes, but will use oranges when he can get them. He also makes our beer and apple cider."

Will was surprised at all the things that were done on the ranch. They were very self-sufficient, but as isolated as they were, they had to be.

"We also have a very good spring," Lainie was saying, "and Juan and his sons have built a wonderful spring house. They built a low building about three hundred feet from the house using rocks from the ranch. We use it to keep most of our daily beverages cool, as the temperature inside it is always very cool. Pipes take the runoff to the horse trough and a ditch has been dug to allow the vegetable garden to be irrigated. We are thinking of running lead pipes to the house and build a water closet, but Juan is in favor of the clay tile pipes. He's not sold on the lead pipes."

It appeared to Will that Selleck and Lainie had found a man worth his weight in gold in regards to the domestic upkeep of the ranch.

Shad walked up toward evening, seeing Will outside smoking a cigar, "These folks live much as we do, Major. Only they got cattle and we got cotton."

"Which do you like best?" Will asked.

"I'm not really sure, Major. The white cowboys treat me fine enough. One of them is even teaching me to rope. The Mexicans are a bit standoffish."

"Texas used to belong to Mexico, Shad, that might have something to do with it."

Shad nodded, "You know I sleep in the bunkhouse. We all do... white boys, Mexicans and me. You wouldn't see that in Georgia."

"No, I reckon we wouldn't," Will replied. He felt restless, maybe even a bit homesick, he realized, as Shad walked away.

One thing seemed to stand out to Will, something that Shad had said. 'I sleep in the bunkhouse. We all do. You wouldn't see that in Georgia.' So coming west was definitely a good thing for Shad. He was being looked at as a man...not Will's man or Will's property, but a man. Sure, he was bound to deal with a certain amount of bigotry and some intolerance, but overall he'd enjoy much more freedom...freedom, not just in theory, but in practice. Will decided then and there, he'd put less emphasis on Shad being his man and more on Shad being his own man. Free to live as he chose and not expected to always be at Will's side. *No,* Will vowed, *Shad would from now on be allowed to come and go as he pleased. An independent man.*

The leaves in the oak tree filtered the light of the moon. A soft breeze was blowing and Will thought that he picked up the scent of grass. Had they been haying, he wondered. The hum of a mosquito was audible, causing Will to take a couple of deep puffs on his cigar to drive the pesky insect away. Walking away from the oak, Will could see clouds moving across the sky in the moonlight. He heard in the far distance a coyote and closer the 'who...who' of an owl. He dropped the cigar in the dirt and rubbed it out with the toe of his boot. He felt his stomach rumble and thought that he might ride back to Austin. The Mexican food that was such a part of every meal here at the ranch was starting to play on his digestion. He'd thoroughly enjoyed his visit with Selleck, but maybe it was time to ride. He'd bring it up at breakfast the next morning.

***

WILL RODE THE BIG BAY to Austin that he'd rode since arriving in Texas. Selleck, Mingo, Juan, Shad, and Lainie were riding with him. At the mention of riding to Austin at the breakfast table that morning, Selleck and Lainie looked at each other and smiled like two conspirators.

"We were just discussing that," Selleck admitted. "We need things for the ranch and Lainie wants to look at some material for curtains. It's also time for a dance or two that usually happen about this time of year."

A wagon was loaded up after breakfast. Selleck planned to ride his horse, but if it got too bad on his leg, he'd swap to the wagon. Austin could be reached by horse in a hard day; taking the wagon added a half a day but it was sometimes best to take one's time.

Looking at Lainie, Will thought, *why rush*. She was the most woman that he'd seen in a long time. While he didn't have any romantic notions toward her, it was apparent Mingo did. Once when they were out of hearing of the others, Will said to Mingo, "She is beautiful, is she not?"

Mingo smiled, "Absolutely, Señor. It is the reason that every hand on the Lazy S is in love. But none of the men dare speak to El Patron about his ward. Not even Ben May, although they have been together more of late. It was thought that you were brought here by El Patron as a possible suitor."

Will thought as they parted, *that's news*. However, neither Selleck nor Lainie had shown any regard in that direction. *I must not measure up*, he thought.

They camped that night close to a fast running creek. "We never camp right at the creek," Selleck volunteered. "Other things need water as well, animals...and men who don't want to be seen."

Will thought this was odd, but didn't dwell on it as Juan announced that the coffee was ready. They ate beef and beans soon after that. *Damn*, Will swore to himself, *did anybody in Texas eat a meal that didn't include beans.*

Mingo went to the wagon after they ate and got out a guitar. He proved to be an excellent guitar player and better than average singer. Lainie joined in on a couple of songs and surprised Will by having him get up and dance with her a few times. The last song had been a very up tempo Mexican song and when it was over Lainie flopped down on her bedroll.

Mingo surprised Will again when, at last, it was time to turn in. He took his lariat and made a circle around Lainie's bedroll. Seeing Will's look of awe, Mingo explained, "For rattlesnakes."

"Does it work?" Will asked.

"I've never had a snake in my blanket," Mingo said. "But who knows? I think why not, it hurts nothing."

CHAPTER NINE

USTIN WAS A BUSTLING TOWN when they rode in. Juan pulled the wagon to a stop in front of the Bullock Hotel. Selleck had ridden the last hour in the wagon but insisted that other than a little sore his leg felt fine. Lainie walked into the hotel ahead of Will, who was waiting to lend a hand to Selleck if needed.

The clerk greeted her warmly and asked if they wanted the same suite. She nodded, but added that they also would need a room for their guest, Major Will Lee. Close by if possible.

Selleck leaned over and spoke softly, "They treat her much better than me." Will doubted this but smiled. "Don't worry about Shad," Selleck added. "I told Juan to make sure that he is taken care of."

After a day and a half on the trail, the bath that was ordered felt extremely good. A bathing room was situated at the end of each floor. One was for the women and the other one was for the men. Tubs were in each bedroom if you had a suite.

The group met downstairs for supper. Will had steak and potatoes with no beans. Selleck and Lainie went upstairs, after the meal, while Will decided to find a poker game. The clerk at the desk recommended the Drover's Rest or the Long Horn Saloon. Neither of the two was as upscale as Scholz, but he was more likely to find a friendly hand at the first two.

Will got directions and found the Drover's Rest first. It was a hotel and bar, just not as fancy as the Bullock Hotel. Will went in and ordered bourbon. Mingo had warned him against ordering 'whiskey'.

"What you get might be what's left from somebody's wash tub."

The bourbon was good...so good that Will downed it and ordered another. He surveyed the room, with his back to the bar. Most of the tables that were playing poker were full, so he contented himself with people watching. Girls in short skirts, showing a lot of cleavage, worked the tables and the customers at the bar. Each of the girls was leaning over enough to keep a man interested in what might be and ordering more drinks.

Will had ordered his third drink when a soft voice beside him said, "The way you're putting that down, it'd be cheaper to buy a bottle."

He turned to the speaker but couldn't speak; before him stood the most beautiful creature. Yet beauty was not the right word. Exotic or intoxicating may have been a better word. Her name was Reida Cohn, a strange name for a Texas woman. Her hair was somewhere between light brown and blonde. It was put up, showing a neckline that a man wanted to kiss. Her eyes were green, matching the emerald green dress she wore. The neckline plunged enough to see the swell of her breasts. Her lips were sensual and when she smiled she had beautiful white teeth. The dress fit snug to a small waist. She was all woman, this Reida Cohn.

Will regained his composure and tipped his hat. "I'd be glad to buy a bottle of your choice if you'd care to sit with me a while."

"I'm not one of the girls," she offered.

"Anyone who made that mistake is plum blind," Will replied. "I can see you don't fit in that crowd."

The woman looked at Will, "Those are my girls."

"No offense intended," Will said quickly.

The woman looked him over, taking everything in, including the wooden hand and Confederate cavalry hat. "Do you drink brandy?" she asked.

"I do most nights," Will replied.

She called to one of the two barkeepers, "Joe, my bottle and two glasses."

They walked over to a corner table and began to talk. Will realized, after an hour, that he'd told this woman his life story.

She was the product of a Jewish father and Mexican mother. Her hair was more on her father's side but everything else, including her temper she said, came from her mother. She did inherit her father's sense of business. He had been a banker before the war. He'd made loans in United States currency but was paid back in Confederate notes. However, after the war, he realized a vault full of Confederate money was worthless. He was being pulled from all sides. People couldn't pay. Markers that he'd signed were being called in. Her mother died from pneumonia, and then the day after her funeral, her father turned his pistol on himself.

She looked at Will and said, "The creditors took our house. He had a thousand dollars in gold and he held half ownership in this place. I made the other owner an offer...five hundred in gold if he pulled up stakes. He signed over his share of the business with no mention of money being exchanged. The creditors tried to take this place but since they had no proof of my father having anything to do with the place they gave it up."

A loud boisterous voice came from the bar, drawing Will and Reida's attention. "Oh no," she gasped. "Not him."

The man was shouting, "Where's my woman. By Gawd, I've ridden a hundred miles to see her."

"He thinks that he owns me," she said. "I've managed, so far, to put him off but the last time he was here he swore that I'd become his wife."

Will was staring at Reida. She was nervous. Mistaking Will's look, she said, "What he actually said was that he'd have me."

"No," Will said. "I don't think he will."

"You don't have to get involved," she said. "He's a cruel, mean man and said to be the fastest gun in Texas. They call him the Brazos Kid."

"I've seen him kill a man," Will admitted.

Brazos looked the room over and finally his eyes picked out Reida. He slung chairs left and right as he made his way to their table. He acted as if he didn't see Will when he grabbed Reida's arm. "Come on, honey, I got us a room."

Reida jerked back shouting, "No."

Brazos, infuriated, grabbed the front of her dress and snatched it in half, exposing her breasts. Will backhanded the man, knocking him to the floor and dazing him. Will took off his coat and handed it to Reida to cover herself.

Brazos slowly recovered his wits. He stood and seeing Will's wooden hand, he smiled. "I have never killed a cripple before but I'm going to enjoy this."

Somebody in the crowd said, "I got money on the major. I've heard what he can do."

Brazos, hearing this, became more angry. "So you're known, are you?" he sneered. "Well, so's a lot of others in Boot Hill." With that being said, Brazos drew his gun. He was fast, some said the fastest, but he was dead before he could pull the trigger as a .36 caliber

Navy Colt slug punched a hole right between his eyes. Everything was silent for a minute, not a person spoke.

The man who had made the bet then broke the silence. "That's twenty you owe me, Gus."

Still, no one could believe it. Nobody saw the major draw his gun. Everyone was sure that Brazos had drawn first, and they were certain that there was only one shot.

Reida still had her hand to her mouth. "Joe, go fetch the marshal," she finally said. She then spoke to the crowd, "No one leaves until the marshal says he's finished." She looked at the other barkeeper and said, "It's drinks on the house."

***

WILL ROSE UP EARLY THE next morning. He felt washed out and drained. His mouth was full of the after taste of cigars and alcohol. He had stayed with Reida until the wee hours of the morning. He left and went back to his room for a troubled sleep. He'd killed another man. He felt no remorse in killing Brazos. He'd deserved what he got from the way he'd attacked Reida. But still...

The marshal said it sounded like self-defense but there had to be an inquest. That meant Will couldn't leave town until after the inquest. He drank some coffee while waiting for his breakfast.

Selleck and Lainie came and sat at his table. After they ordered, Selleck spoke, "I understand that you ran into a bit of trouble last night."

Will replied, "Unfortunately." He then briefly summarized the situation.

"Sounds clear cut to me."

"I agree, General." They all looked up. The man who had spoken greeted everyone. After introducing the man to Will, Selleck asked him to join them. Dan Troupe was the gentleman's name and he was an attorney; a very prominent one according to Selleck.

"I have been asked by our mutual friend to be at your inquest," Troupe said. Will wondered if that actual friend was Reida but didn't ask.

"Oh Dan," Lainie said, "you don't think that there will be any trouble for Major Lee, do you?"

Troupe smiled, "Far from it. He'll probably be given a medal, were it possible."

The conversation turned then to the dance that was being held that night. During the conversation Will realized where Lainie's interest lay. He didn't blame her. Troupe was a tall man, six feet at least. He was slim and had coal black hair and a thin mustache. He had friendly eyes that seemed to miss nothing. His use of General when addressing Selleck showed respect and deference. A gesture that sat well with Selleck.

Troupe turned his attention to Will, before he took his leave. "It seems that we have another mutual friend, sir. Chandler Calhoun and I attended law school together. I haven't had the pleasure of seeing him since the war started but we plan to meet in New Orleans after the harvest this year." He then looked about. "He told me of a particular service that you did for him, sir. That was some doing."

Will smiled and said, "It was as much for my brother as for Chan." He paused and then added, "Our mutual friend talks too much." Troupe smiled but let the conversation drop.

Lainie hinted, later that day, that Will needed some more clothes. He needed more outfits that were readily recognized as a Texas or Western trait and not something that made him stand out as the clothes he now wore. When the shopping was over, he carried his new duds to the hotel and decided to take a nap. It was turning dusk when he woke up. He ordered up a bath after checking to see if the washroom was available. He then dressed and stopped by the barber shop minutes before closing. He ordered a shave and haircut.

While applying lather to shave Will, the barber asked, "You ever think of growing a mustache?" Will shook his head no. "I would," the barber replied. "It would fit you well."

Leaving the barber shop, Will went directly to the Drover's Rest. When he walked in Reida saw him and was amazed at the transformation. He stood over six feet tall in his boots. He had wide shoulders and thick straw-colored hair that had just been clipped. His chest was thick, something she'd discovered last night but with his new rig, it stood out. His arms were long and he had large but delicate hands, or should she say 'hand'. She'd felt the hand caressing her body last night and it felt warm and loving. At one point, the wooden hand touched her, yet even that didn't take away his gentleness. But what stood out most about the man? The first thing that caught her attention last night was his eyes. They were gray, almost a blue gray. They seemed to look right through you, and into your very soul. His new suit set them off as well. Black pants, a gray shirt and black vest with a string tie and a flat crowned black hat with silver Conchos.

He did not wear a coat but explained that the tailor had to make a few alterations. One other thing was different. He had the shadow of a mustache. Would it be dark or sandy like his hair?

Her train of thought was broken when he spoke, "I've come to take you to the dance."

She was lost for a minute. She'd not been to a dance since her father had killed himself. "I'm not sure," she said. "I might not be welcomed."

"You will be or I'll know why. You have thirty minutes to get dressed."

She came down the stairs an hour later. *It was well worth the wait*, Will decided. *Well worth it.*

CHAPTER TEN

WILL SAT AT A TABLE in the dining room at the Bullock Hotel. He'd just finished breakfast and was lingering over a cup of strong black Arbuckle coffee while reading a letter from Chan Calhoun. The other letter had been from Gabby, Brandon's new wife. She wrote that things were going well at home. She and Brandon hoped to have a baby soon and she wanted her gray ghost to always remember that he had a place waiting for him at Eagle Trace. He would never mention it, but Will felt that Gabby's feelings for him were more than sisterly. It worried him so that he promised himself to never be alone with Gabby.

Chan's letter rambled and talked about the cotton market with England. He mentioned all the gossip in Wooten Station, Lee County, and Albany. The biggest being the talk of a railroad all the way to Apalachicola. He ended the letter by mentioning a friend, Dan Troupe, who practiced law in Austin. Will laughed; he'd already made the gentleman's acquaintance and wondered if Troupe had written Chan about the shooting.

The dance had been a wonderful success. The room had seemed a bit reserved until Troupe came in with Lainie on his arm and Selleck behind them. Seeing Will, they immediately went to his table and Troupe introduced Reida as a very dear friend. Lainie was all smiles and the two women seemed to hit it off.

The coroner's inquest had lasted about fifteen minutes. The judge rapped his gavel and got everyone's attention. "It seems everyone knows what happened on the night the gunman, Brazos, met his match. The general consensus is that it was justifiable homicide. Is there anyone here in this courtroom that thinks differently, speak up now?" The judge waited about thirty seconds. "I didn't think so. You are free to go, son. Case dismissed."

The judge then spoke to Troupe. "I understand that your client enjoys a game of cards. You may want to invite him to one of our games."

"I will," Troupe promised.

Outside the courtroom, Troupe said to Will, "That was Judge Joe Buchanan. Don't let his country boy manner fool you. He is a shrewd man and wouldn't hesitate to spit in the devil's eye."

Will had since been introduced to some of the more influential businessmen in Austin. While many of them were influential, only a few were poker players. Will could have won many more hands than he did, but he didn't want to create hard feelings with these poker players. He still won far more than he lost.

The one person to see and understand his methods was Buchanan. "Son, I've known some poker players and some card sharks in my time. You are a poker player and wise beyond your years. There are not many people who would fold with a winning hand. My instincts tell me that you value relationships and good will more than a quick dollar. I admire you, Major, I truly do."

Will tried to see Reida daily and soon he had his noon meals with her at Aunt Fannie's Café. Solid home-cooked meals, and not one time did he order beans.

It was during a noon meal when Dan Troupe came in and sat down. "I've got a friend in Fort Smith who is losing cattle. He doesn't trust the sheriff and it's out of the marshal's jurisdiction. He thinks that he knows who's behind all of it, but doesn't have the proof to bring them to the law. I own a percentage of the ranch and so it's cutting into my livelihood, as well. I have a thousand dollars if you will see what you can do."

Will sat there for a minute with conflicting thoughts. True, he'd grown restless again. Reida was the only reason that he'd stayed so long. He wasn't out of money, but living in the Bullock Hotel was not cheap. Reida had all but invited him to move into the Drover's Rest. He couldn't sponge off of her though. Shad had gone back to the Lazy S with Selleck, enjoying the life on the ranch; Will missed him as well.

"You'll need expense money, as well," Troupe said. "Here is five hundred dollars for that. You can buy range garb here in town but I'd see if you couldn't get the rest of your outfit from General Selleck. I would rather that everyone not know you are going." Troupe handed him an envelope. "I don't expect receipts." Will nodded his head. Troupe left as quickly as he came in.

"He was damn sure of himself," Reida said.

Will looked at her. "Do you not want me to take it?"

Reida looked at Will for a long moment. "It would be easy for me to say no, but I owe Dan too much to do that, just come back to me."

"I will," he replied, and then leaned in to kiss her.

He headed out then and walked over to the general store. The owner was Silas Jones; he'd played cards with the man. Walking in,

Will smiled, "I'm going to give you back some of your losses. I'm riding back to General Selleck's ranch, so I need some range garb. Think you can fix me up?"

Silas smiled, rubbed his hands together, and replied, "The chance that I've been waiting for."

Will bought four pairs of durable canvas trousers, much as he'd seen Ben May and other Lazy S hands wear. He also bought six long sleeve shirts.

"These will protect you from the sun, sandstorms, thorny shrubs, and cranky heifers."

Will smiled at that, "Two legged or four legged?"

"Either, I expect," Silas replied with a grin.

Looking at Will's hat, Silas recommended another similar hat but Will said, "No," thinking of his old Calvary hat. He did buy a pair of boots that was not as fashionable and made more for work. He also bought a dozen bandanas.

"I wonder," Silas said, as he was about to total up Will's purchase. He paused in his conversation and walked over to where his gun case was. Reaching in a corner, he picked up a rifle. "This is a Spencer repeating rifle," Silas said, "An 1865 model. It has an effective range of five hundred yards. It holds seven rim fire cartridges loaded into a tube on the butt plate. This is one hell of a gun. A fellow came through and I gave him $15.00 worth of goods for it. It cost $40.00 new. I'll let you have it and a couple of boxes of ammo for $20.00, if you want it."

Will liked the gun and, though he had the Henry, decided to buy it. When he paid for all his order, he found himself still way ahead of Silas.

"Don't tell what you paid for all of this, Major. I like you and I like your style. You just got everything at my cost and a bit more. I don't do that for everyone."

"Thank you, Silas. When I get back, I'll give you the chance to win back your money."

"You do that, Major, you do just that."

Will walked to the livery stable. The big gelding that he'd been riding had been sent back to Galveston, so he needed a horse. He'd gotten to know the owner of the livery through Shad. He was a free black man named Gordon.

Hearing that the major needed a ride, they walked to a corral in back. "Pick one out, Major. They are all for sale."

As Will looked, he spotted a steel gray, much the same color as Caesar. He was not as big but close. Caesar was seventeen hands tall. This horse was sixteen hands or more. The horse's mane and tail was tangled and knotted. It was not like a livery man too let a horse go like that. "How much is that old gray Cayuse?"

"Now that's a horse alright, Major. I can see that you've got a good eye, but you don't want that animal. He's plumb mean. He'll bite and kick you. He's just not a horse that I'd trust. He was brought in off the range, so who knows what his breeding is. I wonder if he wasn't cut late and that could lend to him being so ornery. I tell you, Shad liked that horse too, and he said that it reminded him of one back in Georgia."

"My horse, Caesar," Will responded. "He is a thoroughbred."

"Well, for a man that could put up with his meanness, I'd say that would be the horse to have. He will run further than most, and he's got stamina and toughness that most horses don't."

"How much?" Will asked again.

Gordon replied, "He's cost me more in feed than he's worth. To tell the truth, Major, I paid ten dollars for him. You give me twenty five and I will throw in a good saddle and bridle."

Will pulled out his money and peeled of thirty dollars. "I want a good saddle," he said.

Gordon grinned, "You got it, Major."

Will, taking the bridle, walked up to the horse and bridled it, easy as you please. As soon as he turned his back to lead him into the barn, he felt the horse start to bite his shoulder. He'd been expecting it. He spun around and hit the horse on the nose with his gun barrel. The animal snatched his head back almost pulling the reins out of Will's hands.

"Whoa boy," Will whispered. He then breathed into the horse's nose and stroked his neck. "We can be nice or we can be naughty. I'll treat you accordingly."

"I've never seen such," Gordon volunteered.

Once in the barn, Will dropped the reins and put the blanket on the horse. He turned to put on the saddle and saw the blanket on the ground. They went through this twice. Will then led the horse to a stall. He tied the reins close so that the animal couldn't turn his head and then saddled him.

"He got a name?" Will asked Gordon.

"Not a polite one," Gordon admitted.

Will tied his war bag onto the saddle horn. He put the Spencer in the rifle scabbard and held the Henry across his lap as he rode out of the barn and over to the Drover's Rest. Reida must have been watching for him as she walked out before he could climb down from the saddle. Before Will could warn her, she walked up and, whispering softly, she started rubbing the horse's neck. They said their goodbyes with Will promising to be back soon.

Before walking back on the sidewalk, she kissed the horse on the nose. "You bring my man back, you hear." The horse gave a little whinny, to Will's surprise.

❦❦❦

WILL RODE UP TO THE Lazy S before noon the next day. The noon meal was good, if spicy. He explained the job he'd taken on for Dan

Troupe.

"It's five hundred miles, or near enough," Selleck swore. "I don't doubt your abilities, man, but you know nothing about the trail. Why that's Kiowa and Comanche territory you'll be traveling through; not to mention the different owlhoots and sidewinders. No sir, I can't let you up and leave, just you and Shad...no sir." Selleck took another swallow of his cider and called for Rosetta.

When the plump little cook came to the table, Selleck said, "Go find Mingo. If he's not around the bunkhouse send someone to find him."

Mingo was found and that afternoon they took an old chuck wagon and made a few alterations. They stocked it with food, cider and whiskey.

"Drink the cider first, else it will sour," Lainie cautioned.

They picked out two mules, a matching pair, and a few tools and water kegs were placed on the side of the wagon. Hoops were put in place and canvas was stretched over them. Ben May then brought more ammunition.

"A hundred rounds for the Henry rifles. It seems like a lot, but there's been times I've wanted twice that much," he said.

Will paid Selleck for everything but the food. Selleck wouldn't hear of that. "When you run out of bacon, you start on the jerky if you haven't gotten a deer to help out with. Trust Mingo, he's the best trail man we have."

They pulled out the next morning at dawn. What surprised Will was that Selleck and Lainie were up and Rosetta had cooked a big meal.

"Probably the last good meal that we get for a while," Mingo said.

They pulled out, with well wishes and warm goodbyes. Lainie even gave Will a kiss on the cheek. "Take care, Major, we care for you here."

CHAPTER ELEVEN

NOTHING WILL HAD EVER DONE prepared him for the trail that Mingo took them on. They crossed the open range from the Lazy S to Round Rock, where they picked up the stage road. That part of Texas was known as the Texas Hill country. Will had noted that the soil was rich in clay. The Hills were cluttered with various types of trees...ash, juniper, live oak. Will also noted lots of red cedar, along with a few bald cypress and mesquite. It was roughly eighty miles from the ranch to the stage road in Round Rock.

Mingo didn't want to push the mules so he limited the travel to about twenty miles a day. The furthest those mules had ever traveled was from the ranch to Austin. Mingo explained, "We need to build up their stamina for the long haul."

They had crossed a few creeks but the water was low and the crossing was easy. "That's not always so easy," Mingo explained, talking about the sudden rains and flash floods.

Mingo would allow the animals to stand in the water for awhile each time they crossed a creek. "It cools their legs and helps with their tendons," he explained.

The first night on the trail, Shad called the mules, Cocoa and Coffee. "They've never been named," he explained. Even so, the mules looked almost exactly alike with light brown coats and lighter, almost cream colored manes and tails. They both had cream colored noses and stockings.

They did remind Will of cocoa but not coffee. His curiosity getting the best of him, he asked Shad, "Why the name Coffee?"

"This mule is docile and sweet, so she's Cocoa. That mule not so much, and will kick if you ain't watching. You've always said that you liked your morning coffee with a kick, so that one's Coffee."

Hearing the conversation, Mingo asked, "And your horse, Señor, have you named it?"

"I thought of Pecos as it was caught along the river, but he's as tough as saddle leather and ornery as the devil, so I named him Latigo." Latigo was the leather that attached the cinch to the saddle.

Will tied him to a rope stretched between two oak saplings the first couple of nights. The third night he hobbled him so that he could be with the mules and Mingo's horse. Latigo tried to bite Will while he was leaning over to tie the hobble and got another smack in the nose for his trouble. He showed no inclination to bite by the fourth night on the trail. He did hump about and buck a bit every morning when Will first got on him.

"Shows good spirit," Mingo volunteered. "Give me a horse with spirit any day...even if he is ugly."

Will had managed to cut a few tangles from Latigo's tail and mane, but he looked ugly being gapped up.

"Don't worry, Señor, it will grow back," Mingo said with a laugh.

Round Rock was a small community formed on the banks of Bushy Creek. There was a large, round, anvil-shaped rock set in the middle of the creek that brought about the name Round Rock. The prairie around the community was filled with a rich fertile black soil. Will had seen cattle, sheep, and even a few goats when riding in. They also saw a few fields of cotton that looked ready to be picked. The town had a general store, café, post office, and a saloon. In one corner of the saloon was a barber chair. The buildings were mostly rough planks with no paint. A few of the houses were made of log.

Mingo thought it would be best to lay over a day before striking out again. "The stage road will be easier to travel," he said. "We'll follow it until we get to the Indian Territory, what some are calling Oklahoma Territory now. There we will follow the old Butterfield Stage route. We'll stop in Sherman and then take Colbert's Ferry at Denison. On the other side of the ferry is where the Indian Territory starts. There's still enough of the Red Devils around to create mischief, last I heard. We'll need to keep watch then."

The general store sign proclaimed the establishment to be Merritt's. The place was well stocked. They bought a slab of bacon, more coffee and, seeing cans of peaches, Will bought three of them. Mr. Merritt told Will that they could set up camp behind the store, if they were of a mind to.

Madge's Café served a good plate and the Round Rock Saloon was good as any. Seeing the Lazy S brand on Mingo's horse and the mules, Merritt inquired as to how General Selleck was getting about.

Before anyone could answer, Merritt said, "A couple of no accounts came through a week ago pushing ten head of cattle for sale. I told the vermin that we didn't buy critters without having a good bill of sale, so they drifted on."

They camped behind the store that night. While Shad was cooking, Mingo took out his guitar. Within a few minutes, a small crowd had gathered. Somebody passed a bottle around. Shad danced around the campfire a bit. Before they realized it, it was midnight, but since they were going to lay over a day, they could sleep in.

When they pulled out two days later, Will was almost sad to leave. They continued northward, passing through some small communities and stopping at others. At Waco, they found a livery and put the animals up with orders to give them oats. Will warned the stableman to be careful with Latigo, him being an ornery cuss.

They ate well that night and stayed in a small Mexican cantina that also had rooms and didn't seem to mind if Shad stayed in the room. At daybreak they were up and, after a quick breakfast, they got back on the trail again.

They passed through the towns of Corsicana, Waxahachie, and others without names, on their way to Dallas. When they made Dallas, they'd traveled about two hundred forty or two hundred fifty miles. The animals looked beat so they decided to lay over a few days. Mingo had an old friend who lived on the outside of town and he was sure that he'd let them stay with him.

Thomas Garcia was indeed an old friend. He looked ancient but was only in his seventies. His stubble of a beard and sparse hair was very white, in contrast to dark brown leathery skin. Will noticed his grip was strong shaking the old man's hand.

Will cleaned up that evening and rode into Dallas to hear the gossip and play some poker. It was a bit far from Fort Smith to expect too much news but the gossip and rumors rode the grapevine along the same trails that the cowboys followed. In Waco, they knew about the one-handed pistolero who had killed the Brazos Kid. Will was sure if he hung around Dallas, he'd hear it too.

In the Ace's High Saloon he found an empty chair at a table where some local hands were playing. "Mind if I join in?" he asked.

"No, not as long as you remember we are thirty a month cowhands having a friendly hand."

"My type of game," Will said.

As the evening went, he was down ten dollars and then up ten. When he hit the up ten mark, he bought a round for the table. They were all drinking beer, so it was cheap. He then lost two hands.

"Remind me not to splurge so quickly in the future," he chirped, getting the laugh he knew he would. He won the next pot and was up five dollars again. "Anyone know how the Fort Smith trail is these days?"

"I hear that the Comanche are stirring things up a bit," a blond-haired guy volunteered.

"Yep," the guy beside him agreed. "I hear tell that they're going to bring the Cavalry back now that the Civil War is over."

An older hand said, "It ain't the Injuns that's so pesky, it's the owlhoots. You ain't planning on riding it alone, are you?"

"No, I have a good Mex to guide me," Will responded.

"Be careful that he doesn't throw in with the no accounts," the older hand said.

Will won the next hand and yawned, "If you men don't mind, I'll play one more hand and then call it a night."

"I'm with you," the blonde said. "Daylight comes early." The other men agreed.

Will won two dollars in the hand and stood up. "It's been a pleasure," he said.

"For us too," the older hand said. "You don't mind me asking, do they call you Major?"

"Some do."

"Well let me shake your hand. You are certainly a gentleman." As Will walked off, the older man asked his partners, "You know who we have been playing cards with?" Seeing the blank stares, he continued, "That was Major Will Lee. He's the man who killed Brazos."

"How'd you know?"

"His wooden hand. It was there in the back of my mind all the time; I just couldn't pull it forward."

"Not surprising, old as you are," the blonde man said.

The other man said, "Well, he sure plays a fair game of cards."

"It's easy when you have his rep," the old man said.

Will had stood just outside the batwings lighting a cigar. So they had heard of him in Dallas. Not what he wanted, he realized, but he couldn't change it now.

CHAPTER TWELVE

IT WAS NOON OF THE fifth day, and nearly ninety miles north of Dallas, when Will's group stopped in Denison, Texas. With the exception of that day it had been a miserable five days. The clouds had started rolling in the morning that they left Dallas. Dark gray clouds scudded across the sky and a good breeze turned into a howling wind. On the horizon, the sky was almost black with the sound of thunder and lightning, causing the mules to become excited and fearful. While the rain didn't come for another full day, the threat hung heavy in the sky.

Latigo started acting up that night and pulling at his rope. All the animals had been tied close to the fire on a rope stretched between two trees. Suddenly the horse started rearing up and pawing the ground, finally breaking loose from his tether, neighing frantically. Soon the mules and Mingo's horse were all acting up.

Grabbing their guns, Mingo and Will ran over to see what was scaring the horses. Shad grabbed a rope from the wagon and followed. Latigo continued to paw and stomp the ground and then ran off. Hearing the buzz of a rattlesnake, Will shouted for Shad to get a lantern. Bringing the lantern, the men saw a dead rattlesnake where Latigo had been tied. The buzz that they'd heard was the last from a dying snake.

"He is bigger than my arm," Shad said.

"Si, and at least six feet long," Mingo added.

Will took the lantern and walked a ways, holding the lantern high and calling to the horse, but to no avail. "Looks like I'll be riding in the wagon," he said, inwardly feeling a sense of loss, as he'd come to like the ornery old Cayuse.

Looking the area over, they found no more snakes. Pulling his blankets over him a while later, Will said, "Makes me want to sleep in the wagon." Shad and Mingo both laughed, but each felt the same way.

The sound of the deteriorating weather woke Will before dawn. Shad was already up, trying to nurse a fire out of the coals to heat up the coffee. Will roused Mingo and then turned to the mules.

"Well, bless my soul," he exclaimed.

Latigo was standing near where he'd been tied last night. Speaking softly, Will walked over to the horse. Rubbing his neck and chest, he bent over to check the front legs for any snakebite marks. Finding none, he rubbed the horse's nose and scratched between his ears.

"I'm glad to see you, fellow," he said. Latigo gave a soft whinny. As he turned to walk away, he felt the horse's lips on his shoulder. He ducked and whirled around, "You scoundrel. I show you some affection and you try to bite me."

Shad laughed, "But it wasn't much of a bite, Major."

It started to mist before they broke camp. The mist turned into a drizzle as they pulled their slickers out of the wagon and put them on. Mingo's slicker was more a poncho that covered his upper body, saddle, and most of his legs. Will's was a leftover from his Army days. It did little to cover anything beyond his upper body and pistols. I'm going to get one of those, Will decided, looking at Mingo's poncho.

The road was a bog by noon that day and travel was almost impossible. They didn't stop for the noon meal, since they were too miserable to even think about food. Mingo was in the lead and pulled up. When Will rode up beside him, Mingo pointed to an old cabin off the road in a stand of mesquite. They rode over to it. The back wall had burned down but the rest looked good. Will and Mingo pulled some debris away so that the animals could be led into the cabin through the burned out section of wall. By the time they were through, Shad was leading the mules around.

Inside the cabin, saddles and harnesses were stripped from the animals. Mingo was propping up some old logs to act as a barrier to keep the horses and mules from wondering out.

"Probably not needed," Mingo said. "I don't think that anything would want to wonder out in that."

Will found a piece of wool blanket that the rats and moths hadn't eaten up and rubbed the animals down. More debris had to be cleared from the front door to get it to open. Once that was done, Shad brought in stuff to cook for dinner. They were all hungry now, as Mingo cleared out the fireplace and got a fire going. The draft wasn't the best.

"Probably has a nest in it," Mingo said. But most of the smoke went up the chimney.

Next to the fireplace was a a steady leak from the roof. They found a bucket to put under it to keep water off the hard packed dirt floor. Before long, the fire had warmed up the cabin and the dampness went away. Shad fixed a rope like a clothesline and the men hung their wet clothes up to dry. Their boots were placed near the fireplace on the hearth.

"That's the last of the oats," Shad said after removing the feed bags from the animals.

They were dry, warm, and contented. After a cigar and a drink they wedged a broken bench against the door so that the wind wouldn't blow it open. They turned in then. Outside the cozy little cabin, the wind still howled. Rain pelted on the roof and lightning could be seen through the cracks in the shutters. With his mind on Reida Cohn, Will finally drifted off to sleep hoping that the weather would be better come morning. It wasn't.

***

THEY'D STOPPED IN SHERMAN TO replenish their supplies. A huge pecan tree sat in the middle of the town. As if by magic, once they rode up to the tree, the rain stopped. The clerk at the store wrote down Shad's order as he called it out, taking a furtive glance at Will and Mingo as he wrote down the order.

When Shad had finished, he looked at Will, "You better pick you out some cigars, Major, as there's only a handful left."

Will picked out a box of cigars that the merchant claimed came from Cuba. The price was a lot higher than in New Orleans. The merchant explained, "They're a lot cheaper in Galveston too, Major, but it's a long way for them to be shipped."

Will didn't miss the man calling him major as Shad had done. He took what was left in one box and another whole box, making the merchant smile.

"I see that you are a man of good taste, sir," the merchant said.

"Do you sell oats, or do we get them at the livery?" Shad asked.

"The livery," the merchant replied.

Will paid the man and walked over to the cleanest looking of the two saloons. It was named the Palace Saloon, but looked far from a palace. He bought a bottle of Kentucky bourbon with an unbroken seal and dust on the bottle, and also some tequila that was in a jug.

"You must not get much call for the Kentucky," Will said to the bartender.

The man smiled, "Lots of calls, just not many wanting to pay the price difference between it and the bar whiskey. It has to be shipped a ways."

Will paid double what a bottle in New Orleans would cost. The barkeeper then surprised him, handing him the tequila. "Cactus Juice is on the house, friend."

Will smiled, "Thank you," and walked out. Shad was loading the wagon when Will walked out of the saloon.

They stopped at the livery and bought the oats for the animals. The livery man was a friendly fellow. "If you need any water, I'd dump those barrels and get it here. There is nothing like it in the Indian Territory."

"We ain't said that's where we are headed," Will said.

"Most don't, but from the looks of things that's where you're bound. There is clean sand near the pump to scour out the barrels. I generally charge two bits for a bucket but since you bought so many oats, it's on the house." Will thought, *I could get to like this town.*

They got to the ferry just about noon, after the barrels were emptied, scoured, and refilled. A sign had been printed with the ferry fees...one dollar for the wagon and mules, and twenty-five cents each for Mingo and himself with their horses. Looking about Denison, Will was glad that they had gotten their supplies in Sherman. The ferry was coming across with a stage but it would be a while. Two wagons and men on horses were ahead of them.

Mingo and Will climbed down from their horses and lit up cigars. The sound of a thump and a dog yelping made Will look up. A large man, so fat that his belly hung down over his trousers, made to kick at the dog again, only this time the dog growled. "By Gawd, I'll make catfish bait out of you," the man swore.

Never one to sit by and watch an animal be abused, Will stepped forward, "That dog bothering you, Mister?"

The man had on a cotton shirt that strained the buttons trying to keep his huge belly contained. He had tobacco stains on his chin and his teeth were yellow. He also had greasy, sparse hair, and his knuckles were huge and scarred. He had been a brawler, Will decided.

"I can't abide his stench," the man said.

"So you kick him and shoot him because he smells." Will's nose had just picked up the sour sweat smell from the man. "He probably thought that he was in good company," Will replied.

Fatty just stood there and stared at Will a moment, like he was digesting Will's words. "You are saying that I smell?"

"To high heaven," Will answered. "There's a river and I've got some soap if you care to take a bath."

"Damn you, nobody says that I'm high smelling," Fatty snarled.

"Some probably wanted to," Will said.

Fatty went for the gun in a worn holster. Before he could clear leather however, Will had the barrel of the Navy colt sticking against Fatty's nose.

Mingo spoke, "They're covered, Major." He was speaking about the two men riding with Fatty.

With the pistol still in the fat man's face, Will walked him backwards to the river. Once they were at the bank, he shoved and the man fell into the cool waters of the Red River. "Splash around a bit, it'll do you some good."

Several people who'd been watching laughed. One of the men riding with the fat man spoke, "Now, I don't say that he didn't deserve that, stranger. But you just showed up Dutch Henry. I have never seen it done before, because he's as mean as they come. I saw him in a bar fight once; he squeezed a man's head until his eyeballs popped out. He isn't one to forget this. You better kill him now or sleep with a gun in hand and one eye open."

"Thanks for the advice," Will said. "I will keep it in mind."

"I'd do more than that," the man answered. "I'd shoot him now."

"You ride with him, Señor?" Mingo asked.

The man hung his head a bit. "He pays better than average wages."

"Not sure that'd keep me," Will replied.

"Reckon I been at it too long now," the man said. He then turned his horse and rode over to where Dutch was climbing out of the river.

Shad was now beside the dog. It was a big dog with tangled, matted wiry-hair. He stood about thirty inches, Will guessed. He weighed around thirty pounds and was obviously off his feed since you could see every rib in his body. He was rust red in color with black down his spine. His pad on one foot was bloody and swollen, and he'd been licking it.

"Do we take him?" Shad asked.

"I don't see anyone claiming him and if we leave him here, he's liable to get shot."

"We got a wait," Shad said, looking at the ferry line. "Let's see if he'll let us tend to his foot. He *does* smell," Shad said, his nostrils flaring.

Will said, "Not as bad as Dutch did, though."

Shad agreed, "No, not that bad."

CHAPTER THIRTEEN

ACCORDING TO BUTTERFIELD'S AGENT IN Sherman, it was one hundred and ninety-two miles through the Indian Territory to Fort Smith and it took thirty-eight hours to travel it. There were stage stations every ten to fifteen miles with fresh horses waiting. It would take Will and his group eleven days. During that time, they'd stopped at a couple of stage stations to spend the night and eat some home cooked meals.

They bought several pounds of dried beef for the dog at the first station. The big fellow was healing fast and even walked a bit on his bad foot after three days had gone by. He seemed to know that it was Will who came to his rescue as he lay close to his bedroll every night.

Shad had taken a pair of clippers he had and clipped away some of the matting in the dog's hair. They'd stopped long enough at the first creek they came upon to give the dog a bath.

"You don't usually see a dog like that on the loose," Mingo said, while Will was bathing him.

"He likely wondered away from some wagon train and got left," Shad reckoned.

Mingo quipped, "'E Señor Major's dog now."

They were about a week out from Colbert's Ferry. They'd just stopped to make camp when the dog started growling. He'd been lying on the wagon seat when he heard something. He was up now, hackles raised and growling with his teeth showing. Everyone grabbed their rifles, and Will wondered if it might be Dutch Henry. Six Indians rode into view after a minute, in single file.

"Choctaws," Mingo hissed and then walked out from behind the tree where he'd taken cover.

The Indians were a friendly bunch, and to Will's surprise they talked about crops, cattle and the need for rain. When one of the Indians realized Will had a wooden hand, he said something in Choctaw to the others. They all stared at Will's hand. A couple of them stood from where they'd been sitting by the fire and backed up.

"They are afraid of your hand, Major. They've heard of the man with a wooden hand that shoots the eyes out of his enemies." Mingo stood up, "Wooden hand says there's no need for fear. He will be brothers with the Choctaw. He will share salt and tobacco, and if a white man does harm to the Choctaw he will come to their aid."

"Major, if you have any more of those cigars it would be a good time to share," Mingo said, while the Indians were digesting his words.

Shad grabbed the box and handed Will a handful of cigars. He passed the cigars out to each Indian and, taking a stick from the fire, he bit the tip off of his cigar and lit it. The Indians followed his example. They all sat back down with their cigars lit. A young brave took a deep puff on his cigar and started to cough. Another brave beat him on the back while the rest started laughing.

Will soon learned that the leader was John Blue Cloud. His brother was Thomas Eagle Man, and the youth was William Spotted Hawk. The braves stayed the night and during the evening Will found out that they all had come from Skullyville. He was surprised how modern the town had been and how many of the Indians had owned slaves. There was even a Choctaw-Chickasaw regiment, but since they'd backed the Confederate cause, things were not so good at Skullyville anymore.

"Bad men came to town. Some stole cattle, and some robbed stage coaches. Some even killed families on the wagon trains."

"Sounds like Dutch Henry."

John Blue Cloud recognized the name, "Him very bad man." Mingo told of their run in with him then and pointed at the dog.

"Good dog," John Blue Cloud said. "He sits like Wooden Hand say. When he moves, he moves like a shadow." After a pause, he added, "I hear that Dutch Henry is at Fort Smith now."

"He got there quick," Will said.

"He wasn't slowed by a wagon."

"Makes sense," Will responded.

The next morning as the Indians made to leave, John Blue Cloud gave Will a necklace. "Tell Walker, Wooden Hand is a friend to John Blue Cloud. He give you help if you need help. You need John Blue Cloud to help kill Dutch Henry's men, we come."

Shad said as they left, "They still got a bit of the warrior left in them, Wooden Hand."

Will smiled, "I think you are right." Turning to Mingo, Will asked about the American names that the Indians used.

"Comes from the Methodist, lots of missionaries," Mingo said. "Before the war, there was even a girl's school. There used to be lots of rich Indians around the area. It used to be a high class social and political center. At one time, it was the Government Headquarters for the Choctaw nation. It's not so much now. Most people have moved over to Spiro. That's why there are so many bad men around Skullyville."

"You seem very well informed, Mingo."

"I have traveled a lot, Señor, and not always on the right side of the law. Nothing big, but a lone steer is very tempting to a hungry man."

Will smiled, at least Mingo was honest enough to admit his past. But if Selleck trusted him, Will Lee surely would.

Shad called to the dog to jump up into the wagon. "You going to name this dog, Major?"

"I've been thinking on it but nothing really seems to fit."

"Name him Red," Shad said. "He's red and you picked him up at the Red River."

"No, I don't think so, I was thinking Sarge, but thinking of John Blue Cloud's words about how he moves, makes me want to name him Shadow."

⁕

PULLING INTO SKULLYVILLE, WILL WAS surprised at all the abandoned houses. Mingo volunteered, "More have moved out." At the stage station, they spoke to Walker, who'd eyed Will's necklace. At the end of the beaded necklace was a piece of turquoise. It had been polished and a face etched into the stone.

"I'd put that under your shirt," Walker advised. "It's considered a prize piece of Choctaw jewelry. Wearing it outside of your shirt could get you shot and robbed."

"I had no idea," Will replied, amazed at what he thought was a simple gift. "John Blue Cloud gave me this."

"I knew that he must have or either he was dead."

"No, he's very much alive," Will reassured him.

The men rode up to an abandoned house that was set back in some ash trees. A lean-to had been built onto the rear of the house and a corral was more or less standing intact.

"I think that we will make this our camp for now. After I get cleaned up, I want to ride over to Fort Smith. Mingo, in the morning you can ride over. I will stay at the best hotel that I can find. If you don't see me, leave a message. Shad, I think someone needs to stay here with our animals and gear. You and Mingo can take turns coming into Fort Smith."

"Are you going to see Señor Ross?" Mingo asked, speaking of Troupe's partner.

"No. While it's assumed that he's honest, I'm not taking anything for granted," Will replied.

Will went to a well located near the front of the house. The pulley block was still there but no rope or bucket. He spun the pulley and it gave a loud squeak. *We'll have to fix that*, he thought to himself. Pulling the board back, he couldn't see anything but black. *Good, it's a deep well*, he thought. He picked up a pebble, wiped the dirt off of it and dropped it into the well. He heard a splash after a second or two.

Shad and Mingo were unloading supplies from the wagon, when Will walked back up to the abandoned house. "We have water, but we need a bucket and a rope and we'll be in business," he said. "Oh, and also a dab of axle grease."

***

FORT SMITH WAS A WIDE open town. Will had already noted several saloons, but the one building that stood out was Miss Laura's Social Club. It was, in fact, a well known brothel. He'd heard a colonel in Braxton's army talk about the place. Before the war, he'd been stationed at Fort Smith, a lieutenant in the Union army.

Will pulled up in front of Goldman's Hotel. A sign said hotel registration was on the second floor. The stairway was made of iron and marble. Will noted four barber chairs and decided to visit one of them after he got a room and had Latigo taken care of. He had bathed at the house that they'd taken over and put on a suit, complete with his black flat crowned hat. He wore his gun on his belt but also had on his shoulder holster. After getting a room, he inquired as to where he could find the livery stable.

Wilson's Livery Stable was larger than the usual livery. It had, in fact, a stagecoach off to the side and Will found out that John Wilson also owned the stage line between Fort Smith and Muskogee.

Wilson was an amicable sort who had a good eye for horses. He shook hands with Will, changing his hand when he saw Will's wooden hand. "That's an ornery looking hoss you have there, sir."

"You've a good eye," Will responded. "I don't know that I've ever owned a better one."

"You're not from these parts," Wilson said recognizing Will's southern accent.

"No sir, I'm from Georgia."

Wilson nodded, "A lot of southerners have passed this way since the war."

The two talked a bit with Wilson promising to take care of Latigo. On the way back to the hotel, Will noticed a wooden Indian outside of Dantes General Store. He went in and bought a handful of cigars that had a Cameroon wrapper. He lit one once he was on the porch and immediately decided that he'd buy more before he left.

One chair was open at the barber shop and no one was waiting so Will took a seat. A barber's chair was always a good place to hear gossip and gather information. A barber quickly asked Will, "Whadda have?"

"A shave and haircut for starters," Will said, rubbing the stubble on his chin. The same old questions arose, where you from, passing through came up and were answered.

"Where's the best place for an honest hand of poker?" Will asked, and got a nervous laugh.

"If it's honest you want, I'd say Bradbury's Saloon most of the time. Also, there's usually a game going on over at Mizz Laura's Social Club."

Will looked up. "At the...ah..."

"Yes," the barber said. "Men don't usually spend much time upstairs. If you're at the tables you are buying drinks, cigars and such. They've got a couple of big brutes for bouncers, so nobody starts any trouble there. I would be careful who you sit down with. Fort Smith is not known as a lawful town. I'd say that we have as many owlhoots, rustlers, and back shooters as any town around."

"Rustlers," Will said, emphasizing the word. "I haven't seen any ranches."

The barber smiled, "You must have come through the Indian territory on Butterfields. Over to the east and north, there's several sizeable spreads. You see a man in range garb but don't never seem to be working, yet he's got money in his pockets...you can bet he's a rustler. They don't ever come in here but customers talk. The feeling is that the outlaws spend a lot of time in Skullyville and Spiros. There are lots of caves around Spiros and we hear that the railroad is going to go through there."

"I saw Skullyville coming in," Will said, lending to the notion that he'd come on the stage. "It looked like it'd seen better days."

The barber shook his head, "The war didn't do it any favors and there again the train is coming to Spiros. There are only a few miles between them." Will thanked the man and tipped him a dollar, and said that he'd be back.

"Name is Chuck," the barber said. "Come on back. We also have a shoeshine boy here most days."

Will thanked him, and with his stomach gnawing on his backbone, he decided to eat and then mosey over to Miss Laura's.

CHAPTER FOURTEEN

WILL ENTERED MISS LAURA'S AND went to the bar. A sign said, 'If you smell yourself, others have smelled you for three days. Be polite, our girls have noses too." Reading the sign, he smiled.

"We get a lot of smiles out of that," the bartender said. "Miss Laura doesn't tolerate foul odors."

"She sounds like my kind of woman," Will said.

"Glad to hear it," a feminine voice said. "I'm Laura."

Will turned to see a very pretty woman standing before him. She didn't wear a lot of makeup like the other women. It wasn't needed. She wore a dress that was cut just enough to show her upper bosom but not near as revealing as the others. She wore a lavender dress that looked like it was made for her body. Her hair was reddish brown and she had big gorgeous eyes.

"You must be Miss Laura," Will said.

The woman smiled, "And who are you? Your speech and dress tells me you're no cowboy."

"No, I'm not a cowboy. I guess if you tied me down, I'd say that I was a gambler but I've been called other things." Taking her hand, he kissed it. "Will Lee, Ma'am."

"A gentleman's words and ways, I've seen the same from many a tin horn."

"I assure you, Ma'am, that's one thing I've never been called."

Laura looked Will over for a moment. "No...I don't think you are. What can we do for you, Will Lee?"

Will was thinking of something witty to say but Laura interrupted his thoughts, "I'm not on the menu."

She mistook his pause as his way of trying to get the words to make a proposition. Will flushed and said, "That was not what I was thinking, believe it or not. I was trying to put together something witty. You, Miss Laura, do put the rest of your...employees at a distant second place as far as looks and other womanly features. But, I'd never dishonor you by being crude."

Laura studied his face a moment. "You know, I believe you, Will Lee."

Will smiled and gave a slight nod, "If I planned to be here any length of time, I would certainly enjoy taking you to dinner."

Laura smiled and batting her eyes, she said, "Why Mister Lee, you're blushing like a school boy."

"I'm sure that I'm not the only man you have put into such a state," Will said.

The sound of a chair scrubbing on the plank floor was heard and a man was saying, "Well, that's enough for me for this evening."

Laura looked at Will, "There's your empty chair. Let me tell you, though, while these are good men, they have deep pockets." She paused and looked at Will, "Good luck to you."

Laura introduced Will to the men at the table. One of the men was Eli Ross, Dan Troupe's business partner, to Will's surprise. The other two men were Foster Byrd and Wilbur Davis. Will took an immediate disliking to Byrd. He had a limp handshake and gave a he..he..he laugh at everything that was said. Yet, that was not all of it. There seemed to be something sinister or evil in the man. Will noticed that he handled his cards well but seemed to fumble when he dealt. Was he stacking the deck? Nobody could be that obvious, or was that an act? Will noticed that when Wilbur cut the cards he never put the cards back on the deck and Byrd always put them back as they'd been cut. He also noticed that each player got a good hand in succession when Byrd dealt. He'd usually drop out and the player that he'd gave the cards to, won.

Will was later dealt three 10's. He kept these and drew two jacks, a full house. He folded thinking something was up. Sure enough, Byrd won five hundred dollars with four of a kind. He threw Will a look, one that Will pretended not to see. *I bet that he's wondering if he'd missed a card,* Will thought.

When a girl brought drinks to the table, Will bumped Ross, who bumped into the drink tray and spilled the drinks on the table and cards. Ross was up and apologizing while Wilbur was scooping up wet cards. A bar towel was brought over to wipe the table and, surprisingly, a new deck of cards. Had the bartender caught on as well? Ross continued to apologize but Will stopped him. "It was my fault. I still haven't gotten used to this hand. Let me buy a round," he said.

Will was up a couple of hundred dollars, by the end of the game. Byrd was up eight hundred to a thousand, at least. Davis and Ross were the losers. *Was that where the problem lay? Was Ross blaming rustlers to cover his gambling losses? It was worth considering.* Will walked up to the bar for a nightcap.

"I see you're no fool," Laura threw out.

"Was it that obvious?" Will asked.

"It was to Harry, who's been watching the game for months."

"Has Byrd been around long?" Will asked.

"A year or less," Harry answered, "When he arrived he was just like everyone else, part of a small wagon train headed west. He was back, in a month or so, with money in his pockets. Several months ago, a man came through from New Mexico looking for his family, who was part of the wagon train. They never got where they were going. Funny thing, nothing was ever found of the wagons, horses, or anything. They had a couple of children along which makes it even worse."

"What does Byrd do now?"

"He claims to deal in real estate, but I've not seen or heard of any buying or selling. He has been seen in the company of Dutch Henry, a real cutthroat."

"Dutch Henry," Will repeated, thinking aloud.

Harry looked deep in thought for a moment, "Mr. Lee, I don't mean to pry, but I see Miss Laura there, sets some store in you." Will waited for him to get to the point. "You wouldn't happen to be Major Will Lee, would you?"

Will thought grimly for a minute, *do they know me here as well*? "Yes, that's me," he said.

"It's good to know you, Major. Anyone who will stand up to Dutch Henry is a friend of mine," Harry said.

Laura didn't look so pleased, "You realize that you've signed your death warrant."

"No, I didn't," Will replied.

"You're not as smart as I thought you were," she said as she turned and walked away.

"She doesn't mean anything by that," Harry said. "She just likes you and doesn't want to see you hurt or worse."

"I wouldn't like that either," Will said as he downed his drink and left.

***

Mingo met Will in front of the hotel the next morning. A few doors down the street, the smell of breakfast cooking lured the men into the door of a small café. The place was packed full.

A man who was walking out stopped and took a toothpick from his mouth, "Don't wait on an empty table. Pick out an empty chair and have a seat. Ma Perkins always seems to know who hasn't ordered yet."

"Much obliged," Will said, as the man put on his hat and walked out.

"There are two chairs," Mingo said, pointing to the left.

There was a chalkboard menu on each side of the room:

Hot Cakes and Coffee 15¢

Ham, Eggs, and Coffee 25¢

Bacon, Eggs, and Coffee 25¢

Sausage, Eggs, and Coffee 25¢

Regular Dinner KC Steaks 75¢

Water Free

Will spoke to Mingo, looking around the room, "Looks like you get fried potatoes with whatever you order."

A young black girl walked over with a coffee pot and two cups. "Ham is out, but we still have a good bit of sausage and bacon."

"Which do you like the best?" Will asked.

The girl smiled a toothy smile, "I like the sausage best. The bacon is too limp for my liking."

Will and Mingo both smiled at that. Will had always preferred crisp bacon himself. "We'll take the sausage and eggs," both men said in unison.

"We got some good honey to go wid yo biscuits," the girl added as she walked off to put the order in.

Once the girl moved off, Will talked to Mingo about last evening's events. "Ross wouldn't be the first man to try to cover his debts by cheating his partner," Mingo said.

Will nodded his agreement but didn't speak as the girl was coming back with two platters piled high with potatoes, eggs, and four links of sausage each. She also put down a jar of honey and a bowl of butter. How she carried it all without spilling anything was beyond Will. The girl hurried off, after peering into the coffee cups, and got a fresh pot of coffee. After filling the cups, she showed them where the pot sat in case they needed refills before she got back.

"It's just about rush time," she said by way of explaining her instruction.

"I'm glad that we got here before the rush," Mingo said with a smile.

The conversation returned to Ross and Foster Byrd. "See if you can find out anything about Byrd's past," Will said. "I'm sure that he and Dutch Henry's gang wiped out the wagon train. I will check on his land dealings." The men then hurried through their breakfast as there was a line just outside the door.

"Let's meet tonight at Bradbury's Saloon," Will said as they parted.

Will went to check on Latigo to make the time pass, and then walked around the town, such as it was. He lost count of the brothels and saloons, but only saw two churches. There was a sign on a building that said, 'Marshal's Office', but the door was padlocked.

He saw, on down the street, a gathering of women in front of a store. A sign declared it to be Kelly & Son, dealers of fresh meat. Will crossed the street, not wanting to get caught up in the gaggle of women. He saw, as he walked down Garrison Ave., a group of men cross the block just down a hundred feet or so. They were not looking his way for which Will was glad. The leader was without a doubt Dutch Henry. The rogue was in town then.

I'll have to be more alert, Will thought to himself.

CHAPTER FIFTEEN

THE SKIES OVER FORT SMITH began to darken. They were the color that Will had heard described as gun metal gray. They were certainly gray with a bit of blue still present. He felt his stomach growl and decided to see if the doors were open at Miss Laura's, but they were closed. By the time he found a saloon that offered a lunch counter, the wind had picked up a bit and had a biting edge to it. A mist started to fall. A man walked out of an office, down the street, and then ducked back in, returning with an umbrella.

Paddy O'Hare's was a large saloon. The smell of lunch being served floated through the bat wings. Like the café that morning, a large crowd was already there. A counter off to the side served ham, sausage, corned beef, chicken, and various other items. Will went to the bar and ordered a beer. While the bartender filled a glass mug, Will asked about lunch.

"Help yourself," the man said.

Will was surprised, but the beer was delicious. Walking over to the lunch counter, Will made himself a corned beef sandwich.

Before he was finished, he'd drained his beer. "Meat's a bit salty," he said to the man next to him.

Smiling the guy said, "So's you'll buy another beer."

No wonder the lunch is free, Will thought, but gladly bought another beer to wash the tasty meal down. Finishing the beer and lunch, Will looked out the bat wing doors. The fine mist that Will had noted earlier had become heavier. *I'll go back to the hotel,* he decided. Just as he got to the hotel, he noticed the building across the street had a freshly painted sign, Land Agent.

Will decided to go over and see Byrd, and see if there were any available properties. He walked in the door and was met by a sixtyish, gray-haired, stooped man. The man was eating and seemed embarrassed that he'd been caught having lunch.

"Is Mr. Byrd in?" Will asked, catching the smell of something foul.

"No, he's not," the man said. "I'm Otis, his assistant. May I help you?"

"No," Will answered. "I met Mr. Byrd playing cards last evening and later heard that he deals in land. I'm from Georgia," he said, deciding to lay it on a bit. "You know that since the war things have changed and it's not the same anymore."

"I see," Otis said. "I will tell Mr. Byrd that you were by."

"Thank you, sir."

Will left the office and rushed across the street and into the hotel. He went over to a window and watched for a few minutes. He was ready to give up when, from the back of the land office, a man rode off on horseback. A fat man. The smell, Will realized, was not the lunch or Otis. It was Dutch Henry. Well, he had connected the two. It was no longer a guess.

***

THE BRADBURY SALOON DIFFERED FROM Paddy O'Hare's, basically by the patrons who visited the establishments. The bar at Bradbury's was mahogany but most people sat at tables. The clientele at Paddy O'Hare's was mostly everyday men who worked for a living. Spittoons stood along a brass foot rail. At Bradbury's a piano stood in the corner, and there was a small stage for can-can girls. The bartender wore a white shirt, vest and bowtie. Both saloons had dancing girls who routinely doubled as prostitutes.

There was a faro table at Bradbury's, along with dice games and poker tables. The biggest surprise to Will was the drink menu which included sarsaparilla, lemonade, apple jack, tea, milk, and off to the side were the brands of liquor and lastly champagne. Will noticed a girl going through a side door, and he wondered if they served couples via a side entrance. There had not been any horses at the side rail. This was probably due to the bad weather.

The heavy mist that Will had walked through earlier continued to make it a gloomy evening. Will found a table and sat down, with his back to the wall. He still didn't feel comfortable with Dutch Henry and his men walking about.

Mingo came in, knocking the moisture from his hat. He found a chair across from Will's and muttered, "Light crowd."

A girl took their order for beer. When she returned, Will gave her two bits and said, "Keep the change."

"Sure thing," she replied. She paused, as she started to walk away, and turned around. "You need anything, anything at all, you call for Madge."

Mingo grinned and Will smiled. "That's a handsome woman," Will quipped, watching as Mingo turned his head and followed Madge's sway as she walked away.

Mingo turned back then, "She reminds me, Señor that I find myself short of funds after buying a few drinks while making inquiries."

Will handed the man several coins that he'd accumulated and then a twenty dollar gold piece. "Get it changed when you can so that you won't be seen toting it."

Mingo nodded, "I have found out that there is a problem with rustling, Señor. I asked with the area being so spread out, where a man would sell stolen cows. The hombre looked at me very suspicious like and said, 'North.' He then turned his back and walked away. Later, I see a half-breed that looks down on his luck so I offer him lunch and a drink. I mentioned to him that I could see he was down on his luck, and then I explained that I had myself been in that same sad shape many a time. While we were eating, I say that I'm tired of Fort Smith and am thinking of riding on, north maybe, but I don't know what's in that direction. He tells me that Van Buren is five miles north of Fort Smith. Since the Civil War, things are bad but better than here. Too many bandits and killers here, he said. I give him a stake, five dollars. He tells me 'gracias' and walks away. I'll find out if Van Buren is a likely place to send stolen cattle."

After finishing their beers, Will asked, "You ready to eat dinner?"

He was not surprised at Mingo's response. "No, Señor, I think I'm ready for an evening with Madge."

A man stumbled in through the bat wings, bumping into Will as he was departing. Will saw a stab of flame from across the street and splinters from the bat wing door flew into the air.

The man who stumbled into Will ducked down and cursed, "I didn't mean to make 'em so mad, winning a few dollars."

Will wasn't hurt, but he paused to think, *was that shot for the man entering the saloon or was it for me. If it had been for the other gent, wouldn't they have shot him before now?*

"Did you see anything," Mingo asked, as he sidled up to Will.

"No, I just saw the flash from the pistol. I don't think that I even heard the sound of the shot."

"I did, Señor. I thought you were done for."

Will walked over to the bar. "Is there another way out? I don't want his friends mistaking me for him," Will said, then jerking his thumb over his shoulder.

"Go through that door," the barkeeper said. "There's a side entrance."

Will hugged the side of the wall, as he ducked out the door, until his eyes got used to the darkness. After several minutes and still not seeing much, he made his way to Miss Laura's. The place was busier than the saloon, but not much. Will took a handkerchief out of his pocket and wiped his face. Seeing the bartender from the previous night, he said, "Evening, Harry."

"Major," Harry replied. "Did I hear a shot a few minutes ago?"

"Not that I am aware of."

Harry nodded, "You better pull those splinters from your hat then. Too close a call to not hear anything."

Will liked Harry so he explained, "I saw the flash but I never heard the sound."

"I've heard of that before from men who were being shot at," Harry replied

"Is Laura around this evening?"

"She'll be down in a bit, but don't you be putting her at risk to get shot," Harry said sternly.

"I wouldn't think of it, Harry. I think too much of the lady."

"Let's hope so," Harry replied, as he walked down the bar to fill a glass.

Will noticed that none of the poker players that he'd played with last night were present tonight. Was it due to the weather or just an off night? He'd ask Laura. Thinking of Laura caused an old familiar stirring in Will and he found himself wondering how Mingo and Madge were doing. He was deep in thought when he felt a soft hand slide along his shoulder and across the back of his neck. He knew for some unexplained reason it was Laura.

"Evening lady," Will said.

"Evening Major, I wondered if you'd be back."

***

WILL WOKE JUST BEFORE DAWN. It took him a moment to focus and realize where he was. Laura laid still, a contented sleep. He could smell her perfume on his skin as he dressed. How he ended up in her room, he wasn't sure. They had been seated at a table next to the stairs. Will had talked with her about Byrd but she didn't have any information he didn't already know.

She reached over, at some point, and placed her hand on his wooden hand. "It must have been difficult," she said. That had gotten Will to talking about his losing his hand. She was not surprised when he told her that he'd been a surgeon. "I knew you were more than a gambler," she whispered as she stood up holding his wooden hand and leading him upstairs.

She poured from a bottle of Martell Cognac in her room. Will had only seen the brand one other time but knew the history and cost. It was expensive. He was sure it was probably a dollar, maybe two, for a glass. At a time when a good bottle of whiskey in a nice hotel ran from two to three dollars, not many people would pay for even a glass of such a rare and delicious drink.

Laura saw him looking at the bottle and said, "I have it shipped from St. Louis."

Will gave a timid taste and then turned the glass up. Laura took the glass, turned the table lamp down and came to him.

***

THE AIR WAS DAMP AND the street was mostly deserted. Will walked back to where the shot had come from the previous night. The ground had been wet from the heavy mist so a set of footprints was visible. Whoever had lain in wait had been antsy. They had moved about and smoked at least three cigarettes, the butts scattered on the ground. It was not a smart person who'd risk being seen smoking while lying in wait to commit murder. Will didn't think Dutch Henry was particularly smart, though, and from the size of the footprints there was little doubt it was anyone else. Will thought of reporting the incident to the law, but he'd seen no lawman since arriving at Fort Smith.

He went to his hotel and ordered hot water for a bath. He also asked about having his clothes laundered.

The clerk handed Will a bag. "Put your clothes in the bag and leave them at the foot of the bed. We will send them to the Chinaman."

"How much will it be?" Will asked, pulling out some money.

"The hotel will pay for the laundry and just add it to your hotel bill." *With a little interest added in*, Will thought.

Will headed to Ma Perkins' for breakfast, after his bath. He was in time to get the ham and eggs this morning. He'd just gotten his order when Mingo walked in. He had a smile on his face as he walked to the table.

Will spoke after Mingo ordered, "I'm going to ride out and check on Shad this morning. You go ahead and ride to Van Buren and then meet me in Skullyville. We'll talk there. I want to see if Ross comes into town tonight. If not we'll ride out there in the morning."

"He may think that he's being spied on," Mingo said."

"That's why I haven't been out there already. If you see any of his hands, find out if they need help."

"Si, Señor."

Will finished his breakfast and headed to the livery to get Latigo. Wilson, the owner, greeted Will at the door. "Headed out?"

"Only for the day, I'll be back," Will told him.

Wilson said, "Just to let you know, someone was snooping around your horse. I might not have known had I not heard a yelp and a curse. Latigo still had a piece of a blue plaid shirt in his lips when I got here. Whoever it was lit out." Looking at Will's hat, Wilson asked, "Is somebody out to get you?"

"Not that I know of," Will responded. "I was about to leave a saloon last night when somebody shot at a man entering. The thought was that he had been a little too lucky at cards."

"They came close to getting you as well."

"I'll get another hat maybe," Will said. "This one doesn't seem too lucky."

Wilson smiled, threw up his hand and walked back to his office.

Will stopped at Dante's General Store to buy more cigars and a hat if they had one. He was tying Latigo to the hitching rail when he saw a man with a blue plaid shirt. He fumbled with the reins until the man walked by. There was no hole in the shirt, so Will walked into the store. After he bought a new hat and cigar, he rode by Miss Laura's and saw one of her "doves".

"You're up early this morning," he said.

She replied, "So were you."

Will smiled and asked, "You're Carrie, aren't you?"

"As I live and breathe," she replied.

"Will you do me a favor and tell Miss Laura that I'm riding out for a while but I'll be back tonight."

"Sure will." Carrie looked up at Will and said, "You sure must be something. I ain't seen Miss Laura take a man upstairs since I have been here."

"How long has that been?" Will asked.

"A year at least, maybe even more."

"She's a special lady," Will said as he nudged Latigo with his knees and rode off.

***

SHAD WAS SITTING ON A bench that he'd salvaged from somewhere, rubbing Shadow behind his ears. John Blue Cloud was there, also. Shadow saw Will and bounded away from Shad. He was barking, wagging his tail, and jumping up and down. Will was quick to notice in just the few days that he'd been gone, the dog had put on weight and Shad had worked on the dog's coat.

"Dog happy to see Wooden Hand," John Blue Cloud volunteered, taking the reins from Will and tying Latigo to a low hanging limb from a mesquite tree.

"Everything quiet?" Will asked.

"We had someone nosing around last night but Shadow started barking and they took off."

Will then inquired as to how John Blue Cloud had been doing and got a simple response…"good."

Will brought Shad up-to-date on things in Fort Smith. He included the shooting but left out Laura. Reaching into his coat pocket, Will took out four of the five cigars that he'd just bought and gave them to John Blue Cloud. While the Indian was lighting up a cigar, Will asked if he knew the white man's word rustling.

"Yes," he answered.

"I hear that a rancher, Eli Ross, is having numerous cows taken by rustlers. Do you know about this?" John Blue Cloud answered again a simple 'yes'. "Do you know where they're being taken?"

"To Spiro," John Blue Cloud replied. "Man change mark there and sell cows to many people. Some of meat goes to Fort Smith, and some goes to the Indian agent."

The mention of Fort Smith made Will think of the butcher and meat shop that he'd seen. He wondered if anyone looked at the hides. When he asked if the back side of the hides were checked, John Blue Cloud only laughed.

"Agent no care, he just want cows."

I don't doubt it, Will thought, and if he'd never been instructed to check hides, he'd never have taken it upon himself to do so. The only thing the agent wanted was a bill of sale to show some clerk further up the chain of command. Will ate lunch with Shad and John Blue Cloud, which consisted of venison, and it tasted good. Shad was invited to ride into town if he liked.

"There's a fairly large community of free blacks," Will said. Shad declined, stating that he was enjoying it right where he was.

Will then turned to the Indian, "I'd like to know who is rustling the cows from Ross. Is it possible for you or some of your braves to watch and find out?"

John Blue Cloud agreed. Will had noticed a .44 Winchester that John Blue Cloud carried. It was a new gun, having been made that year. Will didn't want to ask where he got the gun but the bandolier only had four shells in it. Will walked in the house and dug into his supplies until he found what he was looking for. He returned outside and handed John Blue Cloud a box of .44 cartridges.

John Blue Cloud grunted and filled up the bandolier. He then walked over to his horse, mounted and rode off, without saying another word.

"Think he knows who's stealing the cows?" Shad asked.

"He has an idea, I think."

The sun was starting to set when Will mounted Latigo and began to ride off. Shadow kept trying to follow so Shad put him in the house.

"I know, boy, but he'll be back."

CHAPTER SIXTEEN

T HE STAGECOACH PASSED WILL JUST on the outskirts of Fort Smith. The driver threw up a hand as they went by. Will wondered how much longer the stage lines would stay in business with the railroad coming. He stabled Latigo and then took his second bath of the day. It was after seven p.m. when Will arrived at Miss Laura's Social Club. Unlike the previous night, the hitching rail was full of horses.

Looking around as he entered, Will saw Wilbur Davis, Eli Ross and Foster Byrd. He got a drink at the bar and then walked over and asked if he could join. Wilbur and Eli immediately said yes, cutting off any negative reply Byrd might have made. Will was immediately passed the deck of cards. He felt for marked cards as, Macon Fallon had taught him to do, while shuffling. He soon found marks and by looking at the cards in his hand and feeling the marks he was able to figure out what he was dealt without looking at his hand. The lessons from Fallon had been expanded on by a sweet lady in New Orleans. When he was dealt a good hand by Byrd, he tended to fold. On his turns to deal he distracted Byrd some way and made sure

Ross got a good hand. The first time he distracted Byrd, he spoke of coming by the land office. He'd expected that Byrd would have called on him before now. "You did get my message, didn't you?"

"No, Otis is getting old and forgetful. I will have to speak to him tomorrow," Byrd said.

"Maybe you should," Will replied. "I'm sure that he wrote it down. Funny thing though, I'd have sworn I heard voices in the back, but maybe I was wrong."

The second time that he had Byrd distracted, he mentioned how he'd come close to being shot the previous evening through no fault of his own, mentioning the poker player's words. "Funny thing is," he said, "I walked back over there and found cigarette butts on the ground and where the shooter had stomped around on the ground."

Wilbur asked, "Anything to say who the man was?"

"No, but he had to be a big man to make the tracks that he left."

Ross was up a thousand dollars at the end of that hand. Byrd was angry. He folded the next hand, which Wilbur had dealt, and Ross was up another hundred.

"I came by to see if there's any land around coming up for sale," Will said, repeating the comments he'd made to Otis.

"No, nothing that I can think of," Byrd said, rising from the table. "I don't feel well this evening, so if you gentlemen will excuse me."

"By all means," Will spoke up. "I may come by tomorrow if you are in. I would also like to see your setup, Ross. I want to get an idea of how things are done in the west."

Byrd, almost as an afterthought, tossed a dollar on the table. "Rounds on me before you gentlemen retire."

When the three men approached the bar, Harry set up three glasses and poured Kentucky bourbon in each one.

Ross gulped his down and said, "I best be riding. Come on out tomorrow, Major."

Wilbur bought another round and offered Will a cigar. Will was thankful, as he'd given his to John Blue Cloud. He had just got his cigar lit when a shot rang out. Wilbur rushed to the door but Will grabbed his coat with his good hand.

"Careful, remember I almost got shot last night," Will said.

All the while, Will had a sinking feeling. He knew, somehow, when he stepped outside what he'd find. He was right…Eli Ross lay dead next to his horse, and his coat was open with his wallet gone with all his winnings.

Byrd came into vision, as people gathered. "Who is it?" he said.

A poor job of acting, Will thought.

"Oh my!" Byrd exclaimed. "It's Eli Ross, poor man. I just bought his ranch this afternoon and he'd planned on heading east."

"What was that you said?" Will asked.

"I bought Ross's ranch this afternoon."

"That's funny," Will said, hoping Wilbur wouldn't dispute his words. "He told me not more than ten minutes ago that he'd sell me the ranch."

Wilbur said, taking the hint, "That's so, right at the bar before he left."

"I heard it too," Harry, who'd walked out, said.

"Now, why would a man offer to sell me a ranch that he'd just sold?" Will inquired.

This had the entire crowd talking. "Have you got papers, Byrd?" someone asked.

Another person said, "You better be finding those papers, pronto like."

"That ain't like Ross, he was a good man," someone in the crowd added.

Will gave a brief explanation for his words later, with Wilbur and Harry together at the bar. "Ross did not have the authority to sell," Will explained. "He has a partner and there is a written agreement that should one partner decide to sell, it has to be offered to the other partner."

"Maybe he did," Harry said.

"No, he didn't. I'm the other partner's agent." Both men looked at Will in a new light.

"Hmmm, let's see what sort of documents Byrd comes up with."

"Are you losing cattle?" Will asked Davis.

"Yes, I am," he replied.

"Someone is selling stolen cattle to the Indian agent and to a butcher over in Spiro," Will said.

"Do you have proof of this?" Wilbur asked.

"An Indian's word and he is an eyewitness. Only, he doesn't know the man's name who is selling the stolen cattle. Were I you I'd do a bit of riding and checking hides." Davis nodded and said that he'd take some hands and make that ride to Spiro.

"I also hear," Will added, "that there might be some stolen cattle showing up in Van Buren, but so far that's just hearsay."

"That is closer to Ross's ranch so it'd likely be his cows that have been taken there," Wilbur replied.

"I would appreciate both of you keeping what I told you under your hats for now."

The two men agreed to keep Will's confidence. He was about to leave and then turned back, "Do you know Dutch Henry?"

"Who doesn't?"

"He does dirty work for Byrd. Be careful of him," Will told the two men.

Mingo walked in at that time. Will asked him, "Is that man you grub staked still around?"

"Si, Señor."

"Fetch him if you will. I want this man to ride home with you, Wilbur. If you're able to, hire him as a bodyguard, at least for the time being. I'm not sure if you two realize it or not, but as Laura said to me, "You've both signed your death warrants by siding with me out there.""

It was obvious that neither one of them had thought about that. "Well, it's done now and I ain't about to take it back," Harry said.

"Me neither," Davis agreed.

Mingo returned with his man. "This is Juan Garcia. He is a good man."

"Are you good with that six-shooter?" Davis asked.

Juan's hand was a blur and Davis was looking into the business end of a Colt. He moved the gun to the side with the tips of his fingers obviously impressed. "Don't worry, Señor, it's not loaded. I have no bullets." This caused the men to burst out laughing.

Davis opened his coat to get to his cartridges. "Here's mine. Hopefully, they are still good. Do you have a horse?"

"No, Señor, one has to eat so I sold him."

"Let's go see if we can roust out John Wilson."

When the two had left, Will pulled Mingo aside and told him exactly what had happened. "I want you to ride back to the stage station at Skullyville and, quick as you can, get to Austin and tell Dan Troupe I need him, or papers attesting to his partnership in the ranch, here as soon as possible." Will took two hundred dollars out of his pocket. "When you get to Texas buy a horse if you need too." He thought a second and gave Mingo another fifty dollars.

Mingo took the money and dashed out.

"Do you need a bodyguard?" a feminine voice asked.

Will smiled, "I'd not want to endanger you."

"Nonsense, get your things at the hotel and come back here." Will liked that idea.

"I'll go with you," Harry said, grabbing a sawed off shotgun and putting extra shells in his pocket.

The streets were quiet when they walked out. The clerk, at the hotel, spoke to Will, "You just had a gentleman inquiring about you, sir. I believe that he went up to your room."

The man wilted under Will's stare, "You gave him my room number?"

The clerk swallowed hard and sweat beaded out across his forehead and nose. "He looked a gentleman, sir."

Will, pulling his pistol, ran up the stairs to the third floor with Harry right behind him. They slowed and tip-toed across the carpet when they reached Will's floor. A light was visible shining under the door. Harry stood against the wall next to the doorknob as Will could not hold his pistol and turn the knob with one hand. As Harry leaned to turn the knob, the floor squeaked. The light went out in the room. Harry slowly and as quietly as he could turned the doorknob.

BANG...BANG...two shots rang out. Had someone been standing at the door, they would have been shot. Harry kicked the door open and Will saw a man in the window. He quickly fired two shots and had the satisfaction of hearing the man cry out in pain, slumped half in and half out of the window. His gun arm was out the window.

Will pulled him back inside the room and, reaching out onto the balcony, picked up his pistol.

Folks were crowding in the hall. Seeing the clerk, Will ordered, "Fetch your manager."

Somebody asked, "Is the marshal in town?"

Another spectator laughed and said, "Fort Smith has no marshal."

Somebody else said, "Luther is over in Van Buren."

Will found out that Luther C. White was the Deputy US Marshal appointed to Fort Smith, but he also spent time in Van Buren."

"Somebody better ride over and tell him. We've had several shootings this last day or two. We need full time law here."

The hotel manager was heard shooing people away to their rooms or out of the hotel. Entering Will's room, he asked the clerk, "What has happened here?"

"The dead man on the floor makes it rather obvious, doesn't it?" Harry said sarcastically.

Before the clerk could answer, Will jumped in. "I'll tell you what the matter is. Your clerk," Will said, emphasizing your clerk, "told a thief which room was mine. When we came up, he must have heard us and shot through the door. You can see where his shots busted the door apart. An inch or more and one of us would have been dead. Look at my room. He's tore it apart."

"What was he looking for?" the manager asked.

"Money, you nit wit. He's seen me winning at cards. Your clerk, regardless, gave him my room number and now everything is trashed..." Will then added, "I believe I paid for a week in advance."

The manager looked at the clerk. "Do you deny any of this?"

"No, Uncle."

"Go home," the manager shouted. "Please accept my most humble apologies, sir. I will see that all of your things are put back, your clothes washed and you will be given a new room. No charge, of course." Looking at the way the clerk departed, the manager spoke humbly, "Please understand, he's my dead sister's son."

"We understand," Will and Harry replied.

"I will go get someone to get this...this mess cleaned up."

"You laid it on thick, didn't you?" Harry said.

"Maybe a little, but I didn't want to let on that I thought it was any more than a robbery. Close the door."

Will searched the man's pockets as Harry closed the door. The man had five 20 dollar gold pieces, in addition to paper money, in a change purse.

"He got paid well for this," he said.

"What do you think he was looking for?" Harry asked.

"Anything that might reveal more about me than what they think they already know. Do you know this man, Harry?" When Harry shook his head no, Will said, "I do. He's one of Dutch Henry's men. I talked to him at Colbert's Ferry. I bet he wishes now that he'd changed his ways."

Will hefted the gold pieces and put them in Harry's hand. He made to argue, but Will said, "It's yours, without you I might have been a dead man."

"I don't think so, Major. I was here, remember. I saw it."

CHAPTER SEVENTEEN

T HE FOLLOWING WEEK WENT BY rapidly. Some riders came in to get Ross, taking his body back to the ranch for burial. Wilbur Davis and Garcia were with them. Davis was driving the wagon to transport the body. Garcia was in nicer clothes, no doubt from some ranch hand. His holster had been given a good cleaning and treated with oil.

Will tied Latigo onto the back of the wagon and rode on the seat next to Davis.

"Our marshal, Luther White, stopped by the ranch, Major."

"He came to see me as well," Will admitted.

"Don't judge him too harshly," Davis said. "He has a lot of territory for one man."

"He did say that he's talked to Eli several times lately, and never during that period did Eli mention selling his ranch."

"He's not sure of you, Major," Davis continued, "but he thinks Byrd is nothing more than a four flushing rogue."

"He and I agree there," Will said.

Will was impressed at the ranch layout. It was similar to Selleck's Lazy S. The ranch was self-sufficient and off to the side where a little stand of mesquite stood was a white picket fence. Head stones were visible, as was a mound of dirt that was freshly dug. It was the final resting place for Eli Ross. The hands started gathering as the wagon pulled up. A priest was there as well as several women and a teenage girl. The girl's dress was a better quality than the women's.

Davis spoke; seeing where Will was looking, "That is Eli's daughter, Isabella."

Will nodded his head. He'd not even been aware the man was married. Meeting him at Miss Laura's Social Club lent to that notion. Davis was speaking again and Will missed what he was saying. "I beg your pardon, Wilbur, I was lost in thought."

Davis waved his hand as if to say not to worry. "I was saying Isabella's mother died when she was only two. Her grandmother has lived with the family raising the child. That's her, there."

He pulled the wagon to a halt and tipped his hat. "Zoe, this is Major Will Lee. He has been a recent friend of Eli and myself."

Zoe nodded and held out her hand to Will. He touched the hand and it felt cold. A thought shot through him. Seeing her ashen color and sunken cheeks, he was sure this woman didn't have long to live herself.

Zoe then introduced her granddaughter. "This is Isabella. She has so much of her mama's beauty and her papa's stubbornness."

Isabella flushed and the conversation was cut off as men moved to the back of the wagon and removed the casket.

"Oh, Papa! Papa!" Isabella went to pieces, seeing the casket. Will reached out to get her as she collapsed. The priest took the other arm.

They walked behind the six men carrying the casket, through a gate and into the family cemetery. Several markers were there but two stood out, Mia Ross, Beloved Mother and Wife. The other one was Eli Ross II, You Left Us to Soon. He was Ross's son and died as a child. *Memories*, Will thought. Tragic memories, and he felt guilt again thinking how he'd behaved after losing his hand.

Will noted that the marshal was present, as people gathered around. What was it Davis had said. He was a Deputy US Marshal with a territory too big and with no help.

Will had wondered about the priest when he'd first saw him, but seeing how Ross had married a Mexican, he now understood. He'd never known Mexicans to have any religion but Catholic.

The priest spoke, not a traditional funeral mass, but a good service none-the-less. What did a man need, after all? To live within God's dictates was something few accomplished, but as long as he was right with his maker that was enough. At this point, the funeral was for the family, not the dead. When the service was over, everyone went inside.

In the main room, over the fireplace, was a large painting of a beautiful woman. Will heard a sniff and saw Isabella wiping teary eyes and a runny nose. "That is my mama. She was beautiful, no?"

Will smiled, "She was a beautiful lady and she has a daughter who is just as lovely." Will was called for refreshments in a large dining room that had a table set up like a buffet.

A large man, who was the owner of the general store where Will had bought his hat and cigars, greeted him. To Will's knowledge, none of the other merchants were present.

Wilbur told Will later that Dantes and Ross had settled in Fort Smith at the same time. He then leaned in and whispered, "Eli's best friends were probably the folks at Laura's but you know that they'd be out of place. Eli and Laura go way back, but I've never known him to partake of any of the girls' favors. Laura used to work as a can-can girl at Duke's Diamond." Seeing Will's frown, Wilbur smiled, "It's now Bradbury's. Anyway, one of the local freighters took a shine to Laura and when he asked her to go upstairs she refused, saying she danced only, she was not a saloon girl. The freighter told her that tonight she was. Laura jerked back when the man tried to grab her again. She was able to pick up a whiskey bottle and hit the man in the face. The bottle busted and cut the freighter's face. Duke came over and when the freighter told what had happened, Duke backhanded Laura, knocking her down. He then grabbed her by the hair and dragged her out of the saloon, throwing her into the street. She landed right in front of Ross's horse. Ross got down and helped Laura to her feet. Taking her hand, he then walked into the saloon and shot two or three bottles off the back wall, getting everyone's attention, 'The next man to touch this girl answers to me.' Well, nobody was going to argue with a man holding a pistol that still had smoke coming out of the barrel. He kept his eyes on the bar, but said to Laura, 'Go get your things.' When she came back, Ross walked up to Duke and, without a word, he hit him in the head with the pistol barrel. 'I could never abide scum like you.' Duke wiped the blood from his head but never said a word. Ross took Laura over to Doc's place, and he cleaned her face. We didn't have much of a hotel back then but the doc and his wife said that Laura could stay at their house for a while. Ross, sensing the girl needed to talk and looked like she hadn't eaten, took her over to Ma Perkins' Café. The next thing you know a lot is bought, an old building was torn down and Laura's Social Club was built. It was never mentioned, but everyone knew it was Ross's money that built the place."

Will was surprised in a way, but it made sense. Laura had always been very attentive to Ross. Now that he thought about it, daughterly would have fitted. No wonder Ross chose the place to do his gambling. *Damn*, Will thought, *things are not always what they seem.*

***

AFTER EVERYONE HAD EATEN, LUTHER walked up and invited Will outside for a smoke. A short man was with him. The man, while short, looked hard as nails. His hands were the hands of a cowboy, rough and calloused. His skin was the color of aged leather and he had small beady eyes, probably from squinting all the time. Wilbur had tagged along. Luther pulled his coat off and laid it on a chair. His marshal's badge was bright in the afternoon sun.

Looking at Will, he said, "Alright, we're out of town and also out of anybody's hearing. It's time to lay our cards on the table."

Will held up his good hand and looked at the short man. "I don't believe we've been introduced."

The man didn't extend his hand and appeared to have a hostile demeanor. "I'm Shorty McBride," he said. "If you say the boss offered to sell you the ranch then I'm saying that you are a no good liar."

Will's hand went involuntarily to his gun. His face took on a stern look and when he spoke it was just audible. Wilbur made to intervene, but Will told him no. "Shorty," he hissed, "I will make allowances for your attitude just this once. Since we are now laying our cards on the table, I will admit I lied about Ross saying that he'd sell me the ranch. You see, I happen to know that he couldn't sell it. It's not his outright to sell." Shorty now had a puzzled look. "I said Ross had agreed to sell me the ranch because Byrd said that he'd just bought it. I knew that was a lie. I also believe Byrd killed Ross or had one of his men do it, probably Dutch Henry. By the way, Marshal, the thief that was in my room was one of Dutch Henry's men. Now as to whom I am, I'm an agent for your boss's partner, Dan Troupe, in Austin. I have sent a man in inform Troupe of Ross's murder, Byrd's allegations of having bought the ranch, and what I've uncovered about the cattle rustling." Will then told the marshal about the butcher in Spiro and the Indian agent.

When he'd finished, Shorty held out his hand, "My apologies." Will took it and they shook hands. Shorty's attitude had changed upon hearing the truth.

"Do you think Byrd will push his claim?" Luther asked.

"Yes, eventually. Shorty, stall him, say you are contacting relatives for Isabella and let on that Zoe is in bad shape. You can also let on that the marshal guaranteed you the time and told you that no cattle were to be sold until the deed had been recorded. If Dutch Henry tries to push things, don't try to take him by yourself. Two or three of you draw down on him and fill him full of lead."

"I don't know that I want to hear that kind of talk," Luther said.

"If you're in Van Buren, you don't even have to know about it," Will responded. He then paused to see if there was anything else. He saw Isabella then and continued, "Whatever you do don't let Dutch Henry close to Isabella. I wouldn't doubt what his evil mind would think of."

"We'll keep two men here at all times," Shorty said.

Luther said, "I think you've got things summed up, Major." He then looked at the three men. "I think you've got a handle on things. But, if I hear that there's been a killing this side of the Indian Territory and a body is found, I will have to investigate."

Shorty said, as Luther climbed aboard his horse and rode away, "I guess that means we make sure there ain't any bodies found." Wilbur and Will smiled.

"I think that I will have my friend, Shad, come over and help watch. He can bring my dog." Will then had another thought. "If you see Indians around the herds, don't be alarmed." He then informed them that John Blue Cloud was watching for rustlers.

Mounting Latigo, Will headed back to town. His thoughts were alternating between Isabella and Laura. He'd see Laura tonight, but he didn't think Isabella would have Zoe around for much longer. *That girl has had her share of rotten luck*, he thought. For some reason, it came to him that maybe they should take her back to Texas. She'd do well at the Lazy S, besides, Fort Smith was no place for a girl like her to be alone.

CHAPTER EIGHTEEN

AFTER SPENDING THE NIGHT WITH Laura, Will found himself troubled about her as he rode to get Shad. Together they would go to Ross's ranch. Laura had been very subdued and had asked Will to hold her. During the night, she'd sobbed and at times her body would jerk and shiver.

Would it have been better had she attended the funeral? Will had no answer. However, there was something about a burial that drove home the permanent loss of a loved one. He had witnessed that himself on several occasions. In Laura's case, she had lost not only a friend and father figure. She had also lost both her protector and her financial backer at the same time. He'd make sure that he talked with the banker before he left. Left...the word seemed to shout out at him. Could he leave without knowing Laura and Isabella was taken care of. He pondered the thoughts so heavily that he hadn't realized a party of Indians had rode up parallel to him.

He did not recognize any of them but it was easy to see they were not out for a social call. Will pulled back on Latigo and the horse stopped. He stretched his neck to loosen the reins and pawed at the ground, a sign that he didn't like the situation anymore than his rider. Will reached under his collar and pulled his necklace out so that it could be seen and raised his hand, the artificial one.

The Indians pulled up and the one who had been in the lead spoke, "You Wooden Hand?"

"Yes," Will replied and added, "friend to John Blue Cloud." A couple of the braves spoke to their leader.

"Where you go?" asked the brave who'd spoken before.

"To see the man with black skin and to see John Blue Cloud."

"You come with us," the speaker said. "Buffalo man there with Blue Cloud."

Will was amused at the term buffalo man for Shad, not black man but buffalo man. He didn't think that he had a choice so he fell in line. They did not take his weapons, at least. Will also noticed that when the Indians spoke of Blue Cloud, they didn't add John to his name. Did this mean anything?

The Indians did not follow the stage road but cut across country, a very rough section at that. After riding up over a hill, Will was able to see a small village below. They hadn't ridden much further when Will saw his wagon and mules. Shadow was on the wagon seat tied with a short rope that prevented him from jumping down. *Good thing*, Will thought.

The leader of the band of Indians motioned for Will to dismount. This was not a friendly camp; Will could see and feel the hostility. Shadow started barking and Will petted the dog and spoke soothingly to him. The dog could feel the hostility as well.

When Will turned back, Shad was there. "You've come, good. It appears that some white men came upon the bridal tent of a young brave, who is the nephew of Eagle Man's wife. While the nephew was away from the tent, the men raped and beat the girl. When the brave came back, they clubbed him and left them for dead. The wife is bleeding from below, Will. You need to look at her."

"Me!"

"Yes, I told them that you were a big medicine man."

"Thanks," Will said. He walked in the tent where the girl was and took off his coat, pistols, and rolled up his sleeves. He spoke to Blue Cloud to get some more light. In a moment, Shad brought in a lantern with a reflector on it from the wagon. After Will took a look, he asked for some clean bandage material and his medical kit and the box that had his suture materials in it. Shad was quick to return with the supplies.

The girl had been brutally raped. Her womanhood was ripped and torn, and was bleeding profusely. The area would only heal by suturing.

"I need you to stay and help, Shad," Will said. "I want two squaws to help hold the girl but everyone else must wait outside. Explain that my medicine is better without them here. Oh, and Shad is there any whiskey in the wagon?"

"Yes, Major."

"Bring it in."

Will used bandages to help stanch the flow of blood while he prepared everything. He gave the girl a full cup of whiskey to drink and then poured some over his and Shad's hands. He also poured a liberal portion over the girl's wounds after removing the bloody bandages. She tried to rise up but the squaws held her down. She did not cry out. Will had the girl sewn up in thirty minutes, using Shad's hands when he needed help. He thought it was not too bad for a one-handed surgeon. Before he left the girl, he gave her another cup of whiskey, vowing to get some morphine to help in such cases. The hard part came now.

He called Blue Cloud and Eagle Man to him. "What is the girl's name?" What Eagle Man said was foreign to Will.

Blue Cloud said, seeing that Will didn't understand, "Small deer, young deer."

"Fawn?" Will asked, and Blue Cloud nodded.

"She has been injured badly," Will said, thinking that it was obvious. Choosing his words so that they would understand, he said, "It will be long time...many days, days," and using his hand, he flashed his fingers several times. "Many days," he repeated, "before she will be well."

The Indians nodded, but Will didn't think that he got his point across. "It will be long time before she can be wife again...long time." They got that. "She must heal slowly," Will added.

A shout and groan behind him made Will turn. Fawn's husband had caught on and did not like it. In the poor light, Will could see that the husband had a deeply lacerated scalp, and it needed suturing. He pointed at the wound and spoke, "I will treat."

The brave was called Star. After he'd finished with Star, it was too late to travel. He needed to check the girl in the morning, anyway. Around the fire that evening, he learned that it was Dutch Henry and two of his men who had raped Fawn from Star's description of the men.

"When we catch bad man he will feel much pain long before he welcomes death," Star swore.

Dutch Henry has gone too far this time, Will thought, but didn't feel any remorse knowing what lay in store for the son of Satan.

***

IT WAS THE AFTERNOON OF the third day since Will had left Fort Smith that he rode back in. Going directly to the stable, Wilson greeted him. "There have been a couple of stagecoach holdups since you been gone."

"Which direction?" Will asked.

"The Indian Territory, they mostly took money from the passengers as Butterfield doesn't carry anything of worth, other than the mail."

"Are there any descriptions?" Will asked.

"No, nothing out of the ordinary."

"I see," Will said, offering Wilson a cigar. Wilson declined but took Latigo's reins.

Will made his way to Laura's and wondered if word had leaked that Dan Troupe had been sent for or if this was something different. Will, walking into Laura's place, saw Harry at the bar. He made a motion with his thumb over his shoulder.

"Go on up, you're expected."

Will mounted the stairs and as he knocked on Laura's door, it came open. He saw her standing at the window. She was wearing a pale lavender gown, but what got Will's attention was her face and eyes. They were puffy and swollen. She'd been crying.

"I've been worried sick about you," she said angrily.

Will went to take her in his hands but she pushed back. "I've been worried sick about you," she repeated. He took a seat, not sure what to say but thinking it best to let her get over her anger.

She went over to a stand and poured two glasses of brandy, carrying one to Will. "The night you left, Foster Byrd came in and said that he'd like to buy me out. He offered me less than I have in it, so I laughed at him. He finished his drink and left. Last night, Dutch Henry came in. He ordered a drink and then said to Harry, 'I think I could get to like this place' and left."

"So this is where he was," Will said. Seeing Laura's puzzled look, he explained where he'd been and what had taken place.

Laura had gained control of her emotions by the time Will had finished his narrative. "Poor girl," Laura said. She then looked at Will. "You've never asked what I'm doing here."

"Not my place," Will said. "It matters not to me. It's who you are that makes a difference."

"Always the gentleman," Laura said.

"Not that I always want to be," he said.

"Like when," Laura threw back.

"Like now," Will said, pulling her to him, crushing his lips against hers.

***

IT WAS DARK WHEN WILL walked down the stairs. He'd taken a bath, had a light meal, and was ready to play some cards. Wilbur Davis was at the bar and Garcia sat at a table with his back to the wall. He nursed a drink with his left hand, his right hand in his lap. His hat was off, sitting on the table in front of him, obstructing the view of any person who might be interested in his gun hand.

Wilbur greeted Will to a bourbon, and then joined a couple of others playing poker. One guy was a whiskey salesman named Hardy and the other one was an agent for Butterfield Stage Lines. Neither of them were particularly good poker players but it was honest and a means of passing the time. Will had just won the biggest pot of the evening...eighteen dollars.

"I hear you've had a few robberies," Will mentioned.

"Two," Hayes, the agent said. "Two men wearing hoods but my driver said that he felt like another one was watching. He never saw anyone, however." Hayes then added, "Probably broke cowboys. They didn't even get one hundred dollars on both hauls and that was from the passengers. Hardly seems worth the effort. That's why we haven't been too worried."

A thought hit Will, "I'd not wait until someone got killed to act."

Hayes was silent for a moment, "We've been discussing hiring a messenger...a guard. A man with a shotgun."

Will added, "A sawed off shotgun would be best."

CHAPTER NINETEEN

NEITHER BYRD NOR DUTCH HENRY entered Laura's that evening. The black girl, at Ma Perkins, saw Will the next morning, and brought coffee over.

"Ham?" she asked.

"Sure thing," he said.

She looked about the café and then leaned over. "Two no goods were in here last night. One said it was almost time that you got yours, and when you did he was going to take your hand as a trophy."

"You see them come in," Will said, "You ask me how my bacon was."

The girl paused a second and then smiled, "That limp bacon."

"That's the one," Will said, and gave her a dollar tip.

Will lingered over coffee after he'd eaten. He was starting to feel uncomfortable with people needing to sit down. He'd just got up when the girl called, "Glad you liked your bacon."

Will looked at two hard cases at the door. The waitresses hadn't got it exactly right but close enough for Will to get the point. The hard cases looked directly at Will and then averted their look. As

Will walked by, he made as if he stumbled. He reached out with the wooden hand and hit the first guy in the throat with his wooden fingers, driving the lead man into the second causing him to fall out the door and onto the plank boardwalk. The man's hand went to his pistol but Will stomped hard, hearing bones crack under his boot.

Drawing his gun, Will asked the man standing up, "Do you want to live? You've got about one minute to get mounted and get out of here." The men were mad, so Will said, "Forty-Five seconds," and then he pulled back on the hammer of his gun. "Thirty seconds."

"All right, but Dutch Henry has more than us," the guy standing said.

"He will need a lot more if they're like you," Will answered. "Fifteen seconds."

Helping his fallen partner up, the two men ran to the hitching rail, got on their horses and rode out of town at a good clip.

"Think they'll keep riding?" It was Hayes, the stage agent.

"I hope so, for their sake," Will replied, but he was not disillusioned.

Men like that rarely learned or took heed. They'd leave now but they'd be back with reinforcement most likely.

***

Will lounged around the rest of that day and part of the next. The stage came and went both days with no signs of Dan Troupe or Mingo. Will wondered, had Mingo made it. Had something happened? Owlhoots were not uncommon along the stage route in Indian Territory; or in Texas for that matter. Will had stressed the urgency of the situation to Mingo so he was sure if nothing had happened to him that Mingo had passed the message in all its urgency.

Laura went to supper with Will that evening. It was the first time that they'd been out publically and Laura seemed to really enjoy it. A full moon lit up the evening sky. A gentle wind rustled through the oaks. A chill was in the night air. Fall was upon them and a scattering of leaves fell from the trees, drifting on the air until they finally settled on the ground. A man came riding by on a tall buckskin. It was a powerful looking animal.

"I bet that horse can run," Laura said, making conversation.

"I don't know," Will said, "maybe against a plow horse."

"A plow horse, that's ridiculous," Laura said.

"Latigo would leave that nag standing in the dust."

"You're incredible," Laura replied in a dramatic fashion. "I'm sure that Latigo would give the buckskin a run for its money, Will Lee, but that would be all."

"How about we race?" Will laughed. "I'll even give you a head start."

"In this dress?" Laura said, and then she gave Will a shove backward, hiked her skirt and took off.

Will caught up with her just before they reached the entrance of the social club. He picked her up and swung her around. "You cheated."

For an answer, Laura kissed Will long and hard. When they stopped, she looked in Will's eyes. "Would you take me home to Georgia, Will Lee? Would you introduce me to your brother, your other family and friends?"

The questions startled Will, like a shot right through him. "Why wouldn't I?" Will said, hoping his voice didn't betray his thoughts.

Laura pushed back. "That didn't sound very convincing."

"The truth is," Will said, "you surprised me. Why would anyone other than a farmer want to meet my brother?"

Laura laughed, "I would."

He pulled her close again, having recovered from his surprise. "My dear lady, if you want to go to Georgia, I'd be more than happy to take you. You will be the most beautiful woman there. I'll teach you all the questions that you need to ask Brandon about cotton crops, tobacco crops, and when to pull peaches, so that you'll fit right in."

Laura hit Will on the shoulder. "You're making fun of me."

"Maybe a little," Will admitted, "but you are the first person other than a farmer who has asked to meet my brother."

"Is he as absolutely preposterous as you are?" she asked.

Will become serious, "No, Brandon is a better man than I'll ever be. He is hard-working, a good husband, and a good minister, who cares for people. He would welcome you in knowing what a challenge it's been putting up with me."

Laura looked at Will, her face shining in the moonlight. A tear ran down her face, which she wiped away quickly. "That's very sweet," she said. "I would never ask you to take a brothel madam home."

Will smiled, "Who said you'd be a brothel madam?"

Looking inside, Laura quickly changed the subject. "There are men at the poker tables. Go win some money so that I can charge you room and board."

"I thought I was providing for my keep," Will responded, trying to sound hurt.

"What you have done is set the tongues wagging by every girl in this place. Some are betting that you might even buy the place."

"I better get busy at the tables," Will replied.

Hayes, the stage line agent was back at the table tonight as were a couple of passengers. One had the look of a professional gambler and the other was a rancher. Not wanting to make any unjust accusations, Hayes called out when he saw Will, "Major, would you care to join us?"

"Only if I can buy the first round," Will said.

"By all means," the rancher said cheerfully.

"Harry, give the gentlemen another round if you please," Will said. He then said, "A new player, a new deck..." he paused and added, "If it's alright by you three."

"Certainly," Hayes said. "Maybe a new deck will change my luck... maybe."

The drinks were served and a new deck of cards, still sealed, was placed on the table. The gambler didn't seem to like it much but didn't object. The rancher dealt first and Hayes won the first pot with three tens. The pot stayed small for most of the night. The rancher was probably up fifty dollars, Hayes was down about fifty and Will and the gambler were both about even. Hayes had just dealt Will a pair of queens. Both he and the gambler took three cards while the rancher took one and Hayes took two. The bet started with twenty-five dollars, and Will grinned at the rancher.

The rancher had either gotten what he wanted or he was running a bluff. Everyone saw his twenty-five dollars but the gambler upped it to fifty dollars. Hayes stayed in as did Will. The rancher dropped out. He was running a bluff.

"It's on you," Hayes said to the gambler.

"Two pair, jacks and eights," the gambler said.

Hayes smiled, "I got your other jacks," he said, turning over two jacks and two Kings.

Will smiled; he had three Queens and two sevens.

"You finally had a good hand, Major."

"Thanks Hayes, maybe the rest of my luck will change," Will answered.

The rest of the night was unremarkable until the gambler mentioned a shooting and murder trial in Dallas.

"Who was it?"

"I don't know exactly," the gambler said. "I do know the man is on trial for killing a man who is said to have tried to have his way with the daughter."

"I don't see why they'd bring a person to trial that had killed a man for messing with his daughter."

"Probably wouldn't have ordinarily, but this dead man was the son of some political muckety-muck," the gambler said. "The girl's father will probably get off, folks say. He's got a big name lawyer, from Austin, defending him."

Will was now all ears. "Did they say who the lawyer was?"

"Yeah, a man named Troupe. He's supposed to know the law inside and out."

"He might be a man to know," Will said.

"The man on trial is either hung or free by now, I suspect. That's been about four days ago."

The rest of the evening was uneventful when the stage agent finally said it was time for him to turn in. He was finished in Fort Smith and he'd head toward Little Rock on the morning stage. Will had Harry pour him a nightcap.

The other side of the social club was in full swing. You could hear the girls laugh or giggle as they'd been trained to do whenever a customer tried to be funny. Laura never left the floor for any length of time until all the customers were gone and the place locked up. Weeknights it was midnight and two a.m. on Friday and Saturday nights. Most of the houses in New Orleans were open twenty-four hours a day.

As Will nursed his bourbon, he felt a sense of relief. Dan would never leave a trial for personal reasons, especially one where a man's life was on the line. Looking out the door, Will saw Byrd pause, looking in the door as he walked by. Byrd had said nothing more about his purchasing Ross's ranch, as far as he knew. *Maybe he'd decided to back off*, Will thought. *Or...he may have decided the Social Club was more in line with his thinking. He'd be put straight on both parts soon*, Will thought.

CHAPTER TWENTY

THE NEXT MORNING WILL WAS having coffee when a shadow fell over him. Looking up, he saw that it was Luther White, the Deputy U.S. Marshal. Will had been looking at an old paper that someone had left. Smiling, he offered the deputy marshal a chair.

"Morning, Major, have things been quiet?"

"For the most part," Will replied and told him about the rape of the Indian girl.

Luther acted concerned but stated that his jurisdiction ended at the river. "There's talk of bringing in a judge who'll provide justice for all mankind," he announced. "It's still a few years off, I'd say, but they're working on it."

"It needs to be a hanging judge, a man who will do what's right and not handout a fine and a slap on the wrist," Will said.

"Word is they are lobbying to bring in Isaac Parker. He's a tough, no nonsense man, fair but firm. They also say that he will have the authority to appoint U.S. Marshals. You'd be a good man for the job," Luther said.

"No, not me," Will replied. "I believe it'd take a man with both hands, not just a quick gun."

"You have the savvy," Luther said. "One hand or not, I'd put a badge on you."

"I thought that we were friends, Luther."

"We are, Major, that's why I'm looking out for your future."

"Let me buy your breakfast, Marshal. Maybe with a plate and a cup in front of you, you'll give up on this subject."

A cup and a plate were put in front of the marshal before he even ordered. Pancakes smeared in butter and honey instead of molasses, and on a saucer there were two links of sausage.

"Like you, we knows what the marshal eats," the girl said. "He even puts that honey in his coffee."

Luther smiled at the girl and took a coin from his pocket. "They don't let me pay so I give her the two bits as a tip." Will was glad to see the marshal's generosity.

Luther poured a spoon of honey into his coffee and looked at Will, "Have you ever tried it, Major?"

Will replied, "In tea I have, not coffee though, but I will give it a try."

"It's better if there's enough milk or cream in the coffee to turn it tan."

Will followed the marshal's instructions and took a sip. He decided that it wasn't bad, but it'd be an after dinner drink for him.

***

IT WAS AFTER LUNCH AND Will was playing a game of solitaire. He could never remember having so much free time on his hands. Laura was going over the ledger for bar sales with Harry. She'd said things had been a little slow lately. With both Wilbur Davis and Ross's hands patrolling the range, she'd had a decrease in sales... if that was what you called it. Anyway, there was a decrease in customers.

They heard the horse galloping down the street before they saw anything. When they did, it was Shorty, Ross's foreman. Shorty, seeing Will, almost ran over to where he sat. "Major, it's Miss Zoe. She's awful sick and both doctors are away."

Will stood up. He was not surprised but knew there's little that could be done.

"Go," Laura shouted, "go."

The ranch house was very subdued. When Will rode up, a hand came forward and took his and Shorty's horses. The hand looked at Shorty and said, "She's still hanging on, boss."

In her room, Will found Zoe propped up on two pillows.

"If we take the pillows away she can't breathe well," Isabella said.

"Propped up is fine if it helps her breathe." Will looked at Zoe. "Are you having any pains now?" he asked.

"A deep pain under my breast," Zoe replied. "It's not too sharp, though."

Will thought to himself, *I wish that it was.* Sharp pains in the chest usually had a better chance of living, he was told. "Is Shad here?" he asked.

"He's in the kitchen, I believe," the cook said.

"Send for him, please," Will said. Shad came in a few minutes later.

"I think we'll make Miss Zoe some willow bark tea, Shad."

"It's already boiled, Major. Two teaspoons of willow bark in eight ounces of water, simmered for ten minutes. I strained the bark with some cheesecloth and it's been set to steep for ten minutes. I put a teaspoon of honey and a few drops of lemon in it so that it won't be so bitter."

Will smiled, "Why'd they need me?"

Shad grinned at that. "I done learned your ways in some things."

Will's mentor felt that the willow bark tea was good to manage the pain associated with the heart. He had confided in Will that he felt it may have other helpful benefits that they just didn't know about.

When the tea was cool, they held Zoe up to drink it. She made a face.

"As terrible as that is, I'd hate to think how bitter it would be without the honey and lemon."

Will didn't let on that the honey and lemon part of the recipe was Shad's own addition to the recipe. It did help to make it more palatable. Many had refused to drink it after the first swallow. Will felt if Shad could make it tolerable to drink, it would be more beneficial to the patient. The tea was given throughout the night and by morning Zoe was feeling better.

"Let's cut it to a glass morning and afternoon, Shad. We don't want her to develop a gastric bleed."

The tea seemed to make certain people have severe gastritis, and some surgery patients had increased bleeding when the willow bark tea had been used for pain after surgery.

Shorty came in the house, just before lunch. "It looks like we are going to have a gully washer. The sky is turning black."

Will nodded his acknowledgment. "Is there a time when I can talk to you, the cook, and Isabella together?"

"Now is good for me, Major."

"I'll go get Miss Bella," Shad said and left the room.

"Bella is the nickname that the hands gave Isabella when she was small. It would make Mizz Zoe fume, but Eli liked it well enough and so did the kid," Shorty said.

Isabella or Bella, as she preferred, came in followed by the cook. Shad had called her Lucia, Will recalled.

Will cleared his throat, as the three gathered in the room. It was never easy to tell family or friends that someone was going to die. Lucia asked if she could get anyone something to drink. Everyone declined so she took a seat at the table.

"I am sorry to have to tell you this, but Miss Zoe has a bad heart. I know she feels better and looks better today, but I don't think it will last."

"She's going to die, isn't she?" Bella said.

Will nodded, "Yes."

"She knows it and I guess I knew it, but I thought I'd have daddy."

"Your dad was murdered by someone who will get his just rewards," Will said.

"I hope he does, Major. I hope you kill the...," Bella left the rest unsaid and started crying.

"Don't you worry, honey. You'll not be left alone, that I promise you. Your father's partner has been sent for. He will see you are well cared for, and if he doesn't, I will." Putting his hand over Bella's, she rose up and laid her head on Will's shoulder.

"How long does grandmother have?" Bella asked.

"I'm afraid not long. Let's keep our chins up and make her last few days pleasant ones."

The sound of thunder outside rolled through the house, followed by Shadow's howling. Will had petted the dog last evening and again that morning early.

"Shadow doesn't like bad weather," Shad said.

"I'll go get him," Bella said, rushing out the door.

Shorty looked at Will, "Thank you, Major. Thank you for helping Miss Zoe's pain and helping her rest, but especially for setting Bella's mind at ease in regards to what's going to happen with her."

"No thanks needed, Shorty. I'm sure that you could take care of her."

"No...I don't think so, Major. I know men, hosses, and even cattle, but I wouldn't begin to know how to talk to no young filly. I don't know how many times Mr. Ross said he'd been lost was it not for Miss Zoe."

Zoe died in her sleep that night. She'd hugged Bella and told her how much she loved her. She told the girl that she was the image of her mother, only more beautiful. When Bella went to bed, Will walked over to check on Zoe.

She looked up at Will and said; "I've done all I can, Major. It's time for me to go. You see about my baby now."

"I will, Zoe, don't you worry."

"God bless you, Major." She closed her eyes then and felt no more pain.

"Shad."

"Yes sir, Major."

"Go get Shorty. I want Miss Zoe ready for burial before Bella wakes up."

Shad ran to the bunkhouse and Will went to the kitchen. Lucia handed Will a cup of coffee. Will, without thinking, pulled out a cigar but didn't light it.

"You can smoke in here, Major. Eli always smoked a cigar when we had morning coffee."

Lucia then continued with her chores but Will didn't miss the use of Ross's first name nor the 'we'. Maybe Lucia was more than a cook, and that's why Ross never partook of the favors from the girls at the Social Club.

Ross's will had not been read. It wouldn't be until Dan Troupe got there. Will thought, *I wonder what surprises, if any, it will hold.*

Riders went out to a couple of the nearby ranches and to the priest to let them know of Zoe's death. The funeral was to be the following morning. Will knew that he had to stay but had an uneasy feeling. He'd leave as quickly as he could after the funeral. He couldn't rush things, he knew, but he also felt that he needed to be in Fort Smith...now.

He walked over to check on Latigo with Shadow walking by his side. Had Shadow not suddenly stopped in front of him, he'd have been a dead man. A rifle shot rang out and bark on a tree flew in the air. He'd bent over to scratch Shadow when the assassin had shot the rifle. Everyone in the ranch yard froze except Shadow. He bounded off after the shooter.

Several horses were saddled and ranch hands hit the saddles giving chase. Will forked a pony, not knowing whose it was, and took off after Shadow and the fleeing man. They topped a hill and cut through a stand of trees, dead on the man's heels when the shooter's horse swerved at a full gallop, throwing the shooter onto the ground with a loud 'oof'.

Several Indians rode up to the man. The idiot pulled his pistol but before he could pull the trigger, he found an arrow embedded in his chest. Shadow was on the man now and Will had to call him off. Will walked up to the man but didn't recognize him. He stood back after checking the man's pulse. He'd like to have taken the man alive but didn't blame the Indians.

"He one of the men that hurt Fawn," one of the braves said.

"Take him and give his horse and belongings to Star and Fawn," Will said.

"Wooden Hand good friend," the brave said. They tied the dead man across his horse and rode off.

""There is not many that would have done that, Major. I'd say that was right kind," Shorty said.

Will looked at him and said, "Their kill and their spoils is the way I see it. Besides, Luther said no bodies."

"I reckon you're right, Major."

Shadow smelled the ground where the man had fallen. He lifted a hind leg and peed where the man had been killed.

"I guess your dog sums it up, Major, but I'd like to know why he was gunning for you."

"I'm in someone's way, Shorty. I know the truth about the ranch and about the rustlers. I'm thinking that I should have just shot the sod and put an end to all his dealings."

"No offense, Major, but from what I hear about you, I'm surprised that you ain't just taken care of it.

"Dan would want it done by the book...by the law. That's what I've been trying to do. Knowing is one thing, Shorty, proving it is not always so easy."

"I'd do what I felt was best, if I was you. God and the law can sort it out later."

Will smiled, "I like your way of thinking, Shorty, I surely do."

CHAPTER TWENTY ONE

IT WAS A DREARY DAY. There was a heavy fog or mist that seemed to drift on the air. Certain spots seemed clear but once Will was over the rise and into a level stretch, there it was again. Will had been about a mile from the ranch when he noticed Shadow was following along. Pulling up Latigo, Will got off the horse and picked up the dog.

"Danged if you aren't putting on weight," Will said, getting a lick for his comments.

They had waited on the funeral, hoping that the fog would clear, but since it hadn't by eleven o'clock, they went forward with the service. The priest did a good job summarizing Zoe's life and her love for her family. He brought out that she had been a faithful woman and was no doubt in heaven already. Will noticed that when the priest said that, Isabella smiled a quick smile.

Wilbur Davis was there with his bodyguard, Garcia. The two men still seemed to get along together, and Davis indicated that he intended to keep Garcia on the payroll even after this problem with the rustlers was over.

"I heard that they're still after your hide, Major. You have to sometimes cut off the head to get to the rest of the varmints," Davis offered.

"Have you been bothered?" Will asked.

"No, we've got extra men on the herd so running off the cattle would cause a shooting. It's one thing to run off fifty head of cattle at night. It's another to have men watching the cattle that will shoot first and ask questions later."

Will couldn't help but smile. Davis had a point.

"No," Davis continued, "Garcia thinks they are after you right now. They'll wait to come after me once you are planted. That'll be time enough for me to worry."

Will didn't smile at Davis' words this time. "I might have something to say about that planting," Will replied as he looked at the ash on his cigar.

"I figured that you would, Major."

Will mingled with the visitors and spent time with Isabella and the priest. He felt that he could finally leave without appearing rude or uncaring. Will had Latigo at a fast canter until he stumbled. He had to grab Shadow with his wooden hand and the saddle horn with the other one.

The fog was still too dense and risked Latigo breaking a leg, so Will slowed down to a walk. Will found himself thinking of Laura; when they had walked alone, and her later comments about going to Georgia and meeting his family. She was, Will realized, in love with him. Did he love her? A part of him said yes, but he was not sure if it was love or just a strong fondness. He thought of Reida Cohn. Being with Laura didn't make him feel guilty or unfaithful to Reida. Did that mean anything? Had he not met one or the other, would he be happy with the one he was with? Another question was whether he really knew what love was? Lust yes, but love?

Would he feel comfortable taking Laura or Reida home to meet his brother and family? He would never tell that she was a madam. Saying that she owned a saloon would be pushing it.

Damned if he didn't feel confused. How is it when a person meets two women and has such strong feelings for both of them? What was the old saying, *absence makes the heart grow fonder*. He hadn't noticed any change in his thoughts of Reida. Did that mean Laura meant more? His heart was heavy as he dwelled over this conflict of emotions that had troubled him these past couple of days. He could see, as Fort Smith drew nearer, that the fog was heavier along the river bank but clearer in town.

Shadow was whining, so he stopped Latigo and let the dog down. He ran about sniffing and marking his territory. When he finished, he walked back up to Will.

"You can walk the rest of the way," Will said, speaking to the dog from his horse.

Shadow looked up, turned his head one way and then another and barked.

"Shh," Will said and started Latigo off again with Shadow running along beside them.

The sidewalks were empty as they turned on the main street. Too quiet and deserted. His nostrils then picked up the scent of smoke. Was that a layer of smoke mixed with the fog in the dying light of day. A sinking feeling swept over Will. Dantes was on the front sweeping as Will passed the general store. Seeing Will, he hung his head and walked quickly back into the store.

Something is wrong, Will thought to himself...*terribly wrong*. He kicked Latigo into a run. When he rounded the corner, he could see that part of the social club had burned, the charred board ugly and smelling of smoke. Will jumped off Latigo and ran into the bar, which appeared to be untouched by the flame.

Harry sat at a table. His head was bandaged, and he had a burn on the side of his face. His left arm was in a sling and the right hand was bandaged. He had a bottle in front of him...no glass, just a half empty bottle of Kentucky bourbon.

When Will and Shadow walked in, Will could see that Harry was crying. *Oh God*, Will thought.

Harry looked up and, seeing Will, mumbled in a trembling voice, "She's gone, Will."

Will tried to brace himself, taking a seat next to Harry. He knew that Laura was not just down the street. She was gone so quickly... gone for good. He was just with her a few days ago. "Where is she, Harry?"

"At Bells, the undertaker."

"Let's go," Will said, helping Harry up. Shadow fell in step with the men, as they walked out.

Bell saw them coming and opened the door. He led them into the back without a word being passed. Laura was laid out on a wide board. Her hair was fixed and she had on the rose colored dress that Will knew she favored.

Will took her hand and it was so cold. He held it to his chest and leaned over and kissed Laura on the lips. "I was going to take you to Georgia," he whispered, wiping his eyes. "I...I'm so sorry, Laura."

He saw a smudge on Laura's face as he gazed at her. He wiped at it and realized it was a bullet hole. He stood up, a raging anger building up inside him. She didn't die in the fire, she'd been shot...shot in the face. He turned to Harry, "What happened?" Will growled.

"It was about lunch time today. Byrd and Dutch Henry came in. 'Where's Laura,' Byrd wanted to know. She's not down yet, I told them. 'Call her,' Byrd demanded. I told him to go to hell. Dutch Henry hit me with his pistol barrel then. It knocked me down. I saw the gun under the bar and reached for it, only to be hit in the head again. Laura, hearing the commotion, came out to the head of the stairs. 'What's going on,' she yelled. 'I've come to buy you out,' Byrd replied, patting a paper in his pocket. 'Like hell,' Laura spat back at him. Dutch Henry came over to the bottom step and said, 'Let me have her, boss. She'll be glad to sell.' I was up and lunged after Byrd but Dutch caught my arm and twisted it until the bone snapped, and I fainted. When I woke up I could hear Laura screaming upstairs. I got the pistol and headed up to her room. I heard glass shatter and a gun shot. Dutch Henry ran out of Laura's room with his arms on fire. She'd obviously hit him with the lamp that she kept at her desk. Dutch knocked me down the stairs again. I then heard another pistol shot. I must have passed out again because when I come to my senses, I could see smoke was coming out of Laura's room. I ran up the stairs to her room which was engulfed in flames. The bottom of Laura's dress was on fire but she just lay there. I pulled her out into the hallway and that's when I saw that she'd been shot. It had to have been Byrd since Dutch Henry had run out before the second shot."

Harry reached into his pocket and pulled out a small pistol. "Laura must have shot first, trying to defend herself. Only one bullet was fired. Byrd killed Laura, I'm certain, Major. I've sent for the law."

"He'll be too late," Will replied. He leaned back over Laura. "They'll pay," he whispered and placed a soft kiss on her lips and on the back of her hand. "Are my things still in my room, Harry?"

"Nobody has touched anything on that side of the hall, Major."

Walking back to the social club, Will felt the first pangs of guilt. It was his fault...all his fault. Dan Troupe had wanted him to stay within the confines of the law, so that everything would be done legal-like and above reproach. Laura was dead now because of it. Shorty had been right. Kill the whoresons. He was through with the legal approach. If he ever took a job again, it would be on his terms. No if, ands, or maybes. It was too late now for Laura. He had promised he'd watch over her and now she lay dead at the undertaker's. Will, running up the steps, couldn't help but look in Laura's room. A room that he'd shared with her many a night. He looked and saw the cognac bottle. The label had been burned away and the contents were gone, but the memories lingered. He should have gone to Byrd when he first learned that he wanted Laura's place. He hadn't and now her death was on him. Will walked into his room with Shadow following him.

"Sit," Will said and the dog obeyed. Taking off his dress suit, Will changed into more comfortable clothes. He pulled his shoulder holster out of a drawer and put it on. He slipped his old uniform jacket over it. He checked the loads in both of his pistols and walked down the stairs, with Shadow trailing behind him.

He untied Latigo's reins from the hitching rail and walked down the street towards Byrd's office. A few people on the walkway looked nervously at Will. They quickly went inside a store or office, not wanting to be caught by a stray bullet. Not a person in town faulted the major; even the ones who had never set foot in the social club were angry. Laura, regardless of her profession, was one of their own. You never heard of trouble coming from her place. She was the first to offer a helping hand when needed. For Byrd to come into town with his strong armed ways didn't sit right with any of the town's people. A great many of them felt that it was Byrd that killed Eli Ross, but there was no proof. It was different with Miss Laura. Harry had seen what happened. It was now time for retribution.

The major was an honorable and pleasant man. He'd bought items at several of the stores and was always kind. He'd even bought a jack knife for a boy that he'd seen peering through the windows at them. He didn't know that the lad's father had been killed by a bucking horse. He also didn't know that the mother didn't have the money for the knife. He just saw a youngster who wanted a knife, so he bought it after asking his mother's permission. Handing the knife to the boy, he said, "Every man needs a good jack knife." The boy had grinned from ear to ear. He'd gotten a knife and been called a man all at the same time.

That the major was a kind man no one doubted, but if the rumors were true he had a darker side; that of a man whose actions could be swift and deadly. Fort Smith's people knew that they were about to witness the darker side of Major Will Lee. It was time for the gray ghost to rise.

Will knew, as he walked toward Byrd's office, that there'd be a crowd of men there to protect Byrd. They would be paid gunmen... men who'd shoot first and not worry about the consequences. Therefore, Will must do the same. The time for talking was over. A lantern gave a faint glow to the front of Byrd's office. The glare of a cigarette off to the left, gave away the man sitting in ambush. He'd take him first. If a man was on the other side, he'd have to step out to be clear of Latigo, to get a shot.

Will dropped the reins and pulled out his pistol, Latigo continued to walk beside him. Even at a time like this, Will couldn't help but marvel. Was Latigo losing some of his cussedness or did he sense the danger his master was about to face?

Shadow gave a low growl. He was looking under the horse and could no doubt see the villain. The man with the cigarette tossed it to the ground; and pulling his pistol, he stepped around the building. The Navy colt bucked in Will's hand. The man grabbed his chest and went down. Shadow charged the man on the other side of the office. The man had been trying to get a bead on Will. He focused on the dog now and changed his aim. Will's Navy colt bucked again, and then a second time. The first shot hit the man in the side of his arm; and as he turned Will's next shot punched a hole in his front teeth. Will had aimed high so as not to hit Shadow as he leapt for the man. With the two men dead, Will walked to the door of the office. Standing off to the side, he turned the knob.

The deafening roar of a shotgun thundered out. There was a gaping hole in the door. Will, using the tip of his pistol, leaned around and gave the door a shove, and another blast echoed through the night. Will jumped in front of the door and gave it a kick. The shotgun man was busy trying to feed more shells into the gun. Seeing Will, he dropped the shotgun, with his hand darting to the pistol in his holster. Will shot the man square in the chest. The man took a step back but continued to pull at his pistol. Will shot his pistol twice more; with the last shot causing the man to sit down on the floor. His chest was flowing crimson. He made one more try to get up as his head slumped forward.

Otis sat, off to the side, with his eyes wide open, not believing the horror around him. He raised his hands, "No, please."

Will, seeing no guns on the clerk, holstered his Navy colt. He then drew his pocket pistol from the shoulder holster. He heard the outside door slam from Byrd's office. Will bent over and picked up the shotgun and loaded the barrels with the two shells on the floor. He then walked to the office door and fired one barrel, blasting open the flimsy door.

Byrd was closing a satchel. He looked up to see Will, gun in hand, walking toward him. Byrd's hand reached into the drawer. He never got what he was reaching for as Will shot him in the hand. He grabbed his hand, and as he looked at Will he knew he was looking in the face of death. He wondered, for a split second, if this was how his victims felt. The thought died as a .36 caliber ball punctured his forehead and entered his brain.

Will shoved the body aside and looked into the drawer. A thick bundle of bills was all that was there. He took them out and, seeing more money in the satchel, tossed the bundle in with the rest. He walked outside, feeling drained; and taking the satchel with him, he hung it on his saddle horn. Will had leaned over to give Shadow a rub on the head, when he heard a galloping horse. He looked up and saw that it was Dutch Henry. He swung the shotgun around and fired into the dirt just in front of the horse. With the sound of the shotgun blast and dirt kicking up, stinging the horse's face, the animal shied to the left and reared up. Dutch Henry hit the ground with a hard 'ummph.'

He was trying to sit up when Will shot him first in the left and then the right shoulder. The big man's bone crushing arms were now useless. Will remembered the words of Fawn's husband, Star, as he loaded new rounds into his pistols. *His pain will be long remembered before his welcomed death.*

CHAPTER TWENTY TWO

DUTCH HENRY SAT AS HE watched Will load his guns. His shoulders burned like fire. His head was groggy from the spill when his horse had shied away from the shotgun blast and he hit the ground with his head bouncing on the streets hard-packed earth.

Dutch Henry was still groggy when he felt a loop around his shoulders. He tried to throw the rope off but the pain in his shoulders was too much. He was aware of the major mounting his horse and then riding over and grabbing the reins of Dutch Henry's horse, also. They were walking down the street towards the barn when the slack in the rope was finally taken up. Dutch Henry felt a terrible jolt and he screamed out as he was dragged in the dirt.

People were now coming back out and standing on the plank walkway. Several were pointing and laughing. "Help," Dutch Henry managed to scream out, only to be laughed at that much harder.

Wilson was in front of the barn as Will rode up, "Open the doors if you will, John."

Wilson acted automatically, and with the doors open Will rode in. He loosened the end of the rope from the saddle horn and tossed it over a rafter. He then slipped the end back around the saddle horn. Moving forward, he lifted Dutch Henry off the ground.

Wilson thought, at first, that the major was hanging the man and then realized that he was only lifting him up in the air.

"Steady," Will said to Latigo as he climbed down. He pulled on Dutch Henry until he was facing the way that Will wanted him. He then led Dutch Henry's horse under the man and, when the horse was in position, he backed Latigo up until Dutch Henry was astride his horse.

"John," Will called. "If you will, tie him so that I don't have to worry about him getting loose."

Wilson did as he was asked. He tied Dutch Henry's feet together beneath his horse. Will took the loop from around Dutch Henry's chest and slipped the loop around his neck.

"You try to run off or back up, this rope will do the hangman's job." The big outlaw didn't respond. Will yanked on the rope, "You hear me, Dutch?" The outlaw nodded his head. Will climbed back in the saddle and walked the horses out of the barn.

The stage had pulled up in front of the hotel. Spying Dan Troupe, Will rode toward it. He could feel the stares as people from the town and stage passengers gawked at Will and his prisoner.

Dan walked toward his friend, but before he could speak, Will said, "Your problem is solved, but not before some good people have died." Dan swallowed hard. Before he could form words, Will spoke again, "Go to the ranch. We will take Isabella back to Austin."

"Will do, Major," Dan said.

Will started to ride away and then he paused, "Tell Shad that I'll meet him at the shack." With that said, Will rode Latigo out of town, with Shadow walking alongside and Dutch Henry trailing behind.

Dutch Henry rode in silence. He didn't know what the major had in mind, but was convinced it would be worse than what he had endured so far. He tried to work at his bonds, as painful as it was. *The major is a sly one*, the outlaw thought. He might get his hands free; but the rope around his feet, that would be a chore…well first things first. Dutch Henry gave a sigh and gave up for a minute, after an hour of tugging. His shoulders hurt so badly and he was dizzy with the pain. He'd rest a bit and then try again. His horse stopped and, looking ahead, Dutch Henry felt his last bit of hope fade into total despair.

Several Indians had ridden up and were talking to the major. Blue Cloud made the sign for peace. "How is my friend, Wooden Hand?"

"Wooden Hand is both sad and happy. I'm sad that my woman has been killed. I'm happy because those who hurt her are no longer with us. This man helped them. I would have killed him but thought of what he had done to Fawn. I also remembered Star's words. I would let my brothers get their justice from this one. He is not hurt except here and here," Will said, touching Dutch Henry's shoulders.

Blue Cloud smiled, "Wooden Hand is good friend. We will take the prisoner to Star and Fawn."

Will passed the rope that was looped around Dutch Henry's neck and the reins to his horse over to Blue Cloud.

***

WILL HAD NEVER KNOWN THE type of hurt he felt as he stood graveside at Laura's funeral. Harry had walked up to him afterwards and placed his arm on Will's shoulder. "Major, I've never known Miss Laura to be as happy as she had been these last few weeks. You gave her that happiness, and I'm thankful to you for that." After hearing Harry's words, Will felt less hurtful as he rode away.

Dan Troupe and Isabella attended the funeral, much to Will's surprise. "My daddy really liked Laura," Isabella said.

This was surprising to Will also. "I didn't know you knew her," Will managed to say.

"Oh yes, daddy wanted me to know her and what life held for many of those less fortunate than me. I think he was saying, in a way, if you're not careful you could end up like these soiled doves."

Dan Troupe spoke then, changing the subject, obviously from one he wasn't comfortable with. "I have a letter for you, Major, from a lady." *Reida*, Will thought, with a tinge of guilt.

He'd felt a lot of guilt lately, but he'd felt no guilt over delivering Dutch Henry to the Choctaws. Their justice was such that a man would think long and hard before raping one of their women. Dutch Henry had been left in a place along the trail as a warning to all of the consequences for rape. The squaws were particularly adept at torture. Will could still see an image in his mind where a fire had been built over the rapist's private parts. The words 'welcome death' had a new meaning. Yet Will could find no sorrow for Dutch Henry.

Shad was at the house when Will rode up. "It's good to see you, Will," Shad said. "I've been worried about you." Shad said. Calling Will by his first name told Will two things. One, they were alone, no one else was at the cabin; and two, Shad understood the hurt and conflict of emotions that Will was going through. The two men talked over a warm fire and glass of brandy.

"You know, sometimes we just get caught up in something that takes you further than you ever intended," Shad said. "I suspect that other than Mr. Ross, who was a father-like man, you were the first gentleman who ever gave Miss Laura any attention that wasn't a proposition. I expect, Will, that Mr. Harry was right. You brought that girl more happiness that she'd had in a long spell. Maybe more than she'd ever had. She's gone now and you ain't. You've made sure justice was served. Now it's time to move on."

"But if she'd lived," Will began.

Shad held up his hand. "She didn't, she's gone. There's no reason to think about what ifs. Read your letter from Miss Reida." Will nodded, knowing Shad was right.

"Will."

"Yes."

"There's no need for you to go making Miss Reida upset by talking about Miss. Laura. Things are better left alone sometimes."

"She'll hear that I killed those men..."

"For what they did to Mr. Ross and his lady friend," Shad said, interrupting Will.

Will nodded and dug out Reida's letter.

EPILOGUE

THE TRIP BACK TO AUSTIN was uneventful. Will and Mingo made the trip back together with Shad, not wanting him to travel by himself. Dan and Isabella took the stage back.

The morning they pulled out, Latigo tried to bite Will as he bent over to pick up the saddle. "You damned old crow bait," Will shouted. "I'll bust you a good one, you do that again." His shout caused Shadow to bark at Latigo. Mingo and Shad couldn't help but laugh at the outburst.

When they got to the cut off trail that led to the Lazy S, Shad and Mingo headed toward the ranch, while Will headed to Austin. When he pulled up in front of the Drover's Rest, he felt tightness in his chest. He had misgivings about not telling Reida about Laura. Was Shad right? There was no need to bring up something that was sure to be hurtful.

His thoughts were interrupted by a slightly husky voice, "Are you going to stand there by your horse all night or are you coming in?"

Will smiled, "I'm coming in."

Reida was through the bat wings and embracing Will before he could speak further. After a long passionate kiss, Reida took him by the hand leading him to her table. A bottle of bourbon and two glasses were brought over.

"Word is that you've been through a lot, Will." He felt his chest heave. She laid her hand on his and seeing the look in his eyes, she spoke again. "Word travels fast. Everyone is talking about the major with the wooden hand ridding Fort Smith of murderers and rustlers."

Will went to speak, but Reida put her finger over his lips. "Drink up and come with me."

The next morning, Will woke up to the crowing of a rooster nearby. Reida still slept on. She had kissed him, after they'd made love, and said, "I love you, Will Lee, but I put no demands on you. What happens when you are away working stays away, as long as you come back to me when the job is over."

"Who says I'll take another job?"

Reida sat up making Will's eyes widen. Reida shoved him down on the bed, "You will, you always will. You get results."

A few days later, Will was sitting on the front porch at the Bullock Hotel. A voice called out, "It's Major Lee." Will looked up and there was Bella, Lainie, and William Selleck. Will stood and Bella ran to him, giving him a big hug.

"How do you like Texas?" Will asked when the girl finally let go.

"It's great," she responded. "Miss Lainie and Mr. Selleck are so nice, but I do miss some of our hands, especially Shorty."

"Be sure that you write him," Will offered.

"I already have. I've missed you too, Uncle Will." Seeing the surprise on Will's face at her calling him Uncle, Bella asked, "You don't mind me calling you uncle, do you?"

"Of course not," Will answered. "In fact, I like the idea."

Selleck spoke then, "It's Bella's birthday, so the girls are going to do a little shopping, Major."

Will laughed, "A woman's favorite pastime."

Selleck walked over to a rocking chair, as the women walked into the hotel. Reaching into his pocket, he brought out two cigars. "It's too early for a drink, Major, so let's enjoy one of these."

After they had both lit their cigars and had a good plume of smoke rising, Selleck spoke again, "Have you recovered from your trip, Major?"

"Pretty much, it seems that all I've done is eat, sleep, and play poker."

"Good," Selleck replied. "I've a job for you, Major. One that is right up your line. It pays one thousand dollars and expenses."

"When do I need to leave?"

"Is your horse saddled?"

About the Author

MICHAEL AYE IS A RETIRED Naval Medical Officer. As a child, he was a fan of the comic Western heroes. When he grew older, he started reading the masters of the Western genre. Lewis B. Patten, Jonas Ward, Luke Short and Louis L'Amour were his favorites. Michael spent many hours reading Westerns, often trading books with shipmates while at sea. Michael is a student of early American and British Naval history and has written many maritime fiction novels under the pen name of Michael Aye. *The Rise of the Gray Ghost* is his first western.